"Joe Koch belongs in any conversation featuring the likes of Livia Llewellyn or Michael Cisco, but is incomparable. Dizzyingly inventive, and weird as weird gets, *Invaginies* will floor everybody."

— LAIRD BARRON, AUTHOR OF *NOT A SPECK OF LIGHT* (STORIES)

"Seductively cerebral. Joe Koch peels away the world you know to show a deeper one you can't unsee. There's no recovering from *Invaginies*. This book digs into your head and makes you fall in love, even as it eats your brain from the inside out."

— HAILEY PIPER, BRAM STOKER AWARD-WINNING AUTHOR OF *QUEEN OF TEETH*

"A thought-provoking collection that readers will experience physically, making it a great suggestion for those who like to mix their literary fiction with visceral, lush prose, recounting stories that captivate and discomfort in equal measure."

— *BOOKLIST*

"*Invaginies* is Koch's nastiest and most formally daring collection yet, a glistening tangle of poetic viscera dragged out into the light and impossible to look away from."

— GRETCHEN FELKER-MARTIN, AUTHOR OF *MANHUNT*

"Joe Koch's new collection *Invaginies* disturbs and disorients with each turning page, the dread of each new vision escalating until the book fairly throbs in your trembling hands. Koch's language, precise and unyielding, illuminates each cruel moment like flashes of lightning, striking ever closer until the heat, the brilliance, the smell of sizzling flesh envelops you. Like the razor in Un Chien Andalou, each story is honed to a gleaming edge and slices keenly into the reader's understanding of themselves and the world they thought they knew. This is the darkest art, and Joe Koch is its master."

— DAVID DEMCHUK, AWARD-WINNING
AUTHOR OF *THE BONE MOTHER* AND
RED X

"I'm awestruck by Joe Koch's nonstop spellbinding, almost paralyzingly inventive and yet propulsive, ultra-focused prose."

— DENNIS COOPER, AUTHOR OF *THE
MARBLED SWARM, I WISHED, THE SLUTS*

INVAGINIES

HORROR

To the weirdos and the queers.

CONTENTS

INVAGINIES

JOE KOCH

CLASH
HORROR

INVAGINIES

Gnawing a new nipple door into the afterlife, the first breaks free by annihilation. You're left behind with the second and third, our rankings bumped up by one cage as the caretakers move each participant closer to the crime. As the new number one, you think you know what you will become. You've witnessed those before you protest violence with violence, face repetition with resistance, and then, as the last door closed on them with nowhere left to go but the inside of the cell, you knew them in contrast, no longer colored by gradations. You tell yourself you'll answer the cubed microscopic view of Vantablack salt restructuring your cells with naked light.

The purpose of capitalism is to make more bodies. You, the new number one with your face like the city, the city we can't remember where the queerest drug addicts argue on the street; you with your mutable proliferation of breasts smothering every revolutionary impulse; you, one cage ahead of me, laser scoping a red dot, red eye pinpoint of light aimed through a windshield chasing a dancer with untranslatable emotions. Moving and ephemeral or solid, her torture garden of outdated GPS drop pins in historical labia. Sickness is stillness. War is health. The city needs war to keep moving.

At this stage in our treatment, you and I understand the city has declared war on our bodies.

There's a building outside our window that looks like a burning candle. You come to realize I am watching you closely as I take a shit in the corner of my adjoining cell. I tell you someday I am going to fuck this building so hard it falls down. I'm going to make my body a black cube and attack you like a gun with no orifice. I'm going to rescue you and kidnap the dancer and find the field that grows the war.

I tell you we're going for a ride someday and there's nothing you can do to slow this baby down. When I find the war I will break it into pieces small enough for us to swallow. This treatment plan is a metaphor for forced birth.

One cage ahead of me, you're a motorcycle with a subconscious desire to fly. Your design screams for infection. I'm cold beneath you, endemic in the concrete. I inhabit spaces so brutal I've evolved into a sentient disease. When I disappear into the 1970s, I'll take you with me to find the best cocaine-and-flower-patterned contact paper ever copied. I will make my body a white cube of salt that burns on your tongue.

Disease is a double agent in the war. I'm whispering to you, the new number one. The doctor is in. The doctor is in the walls. The doctor is in the walls of our cells and the clanging of our armored doors. When your mother comes to visit, you tell her you're getting better and she says you're such a good boy. I'm the only one who knows you're lying. I can sublimate with the best of them. The doctor is in your mouth.

I want to cry for you and your soft sympathetic mother, but I can't cry anymore since I came to the crystalline city of Vantablack salt. Black cubes like stacked cars propel a war nobody else remembers. Space structured around acceleration begs fertility of concrete. The city needs bodies to make more capitalism and we are not piled high enough to accrete a convincing geology. Time in this habitat is a moving microscopic image of the inside of my colon. Here I show you the wet slippery place where I look for you when you turn away from me in your cage.

You so often turn away.

As the new number one, you precede my silence with your clamor of slippery tears and a torture spread of imaginary geography: we are the map. I can't cry anymore, no matter how hard I try. I watch you closely as I crouch and take a shit in my adjoining cell and try to feel you working your way out from inside. This view of the severe angles of your interior cell wall corrupts my emotions. Nobody talks about the war, as if you and I were two separate subjects in a compulsory study of sensory deprivation and sibling rivalry instead of a conjoined monument to progress.

I masturbate while I watch you, unable to come, wishing you were back here in my colon where my anatomy could shape you properly. The number joke becomes distasteful and obvious in this context, an unintentional slander against your name. The real joke is that we've always been free to leave this facility any time we've wanted.

You can't start a joke with the punchline. That's like a nautilus trying to build a home from the outside of the shell inward, enfolding smaller anachronistic chambers before they exist in the logarithmic spiral. You have to tell a joke in the correct linear order. Two veterans walk into a bathtub. An invisible doctor and an overcoat walk out of thin air. A mechanic, a helicopter, and a commodity walk into a heist. Nobody talks about the war.

The doctor is in. The doctor is in the space between your body's relationship with disease and the paranoid claustrophobia of a weaker mind, in the forced birth of shining wet places collecting like polyps in your bleeding mouth, in the air pockets of lifeless concrete where I conceptualize my rebirth as an apocalyptic infection.

I dream of the day when we run away together, brother, and redefine your pregnancies to fit the shape of a collective revolutionary orifice in sickness and in health. Our bodies will create a vehicle with a sleek Vantablack carapace that slides through the dangerous corridors of a city we've never seen except through our recovered memories, a city in queer time. In the trauma of my nightmares, it is constructed like a series of slipping cubes.

The doctor is in. The doctor is inside us, taking shape in our bowels. I mime him like a wild homunculus from my cage for your horrified edification, my limbs of shit writhing, kneading, and pleading with you to let me feel something. If I turn into a cube for you, will you let me cry again? Will you slip me back my health on the sly, dear doctor, like a drug deal? Will you let me come again, dear brother, and ooze evidence of how far we have evolved since conception?

Through clenched teeth of disgust you say it's your duty to remind me that this is a voluntary study. It's as if you presume a fellow doctor is a commodity, like a work of art. You can buy and sell me like one of your extraneous agents, but we both know disease is the ultimate secret weapon and birth is nothing but a cover-up. I can't mend a mind that isn't broken. Give me your shoes and I'll show how much more I can collapse of the visible dark. Give me your hands and your credentials and close your eyes so that I may silently feed you the war broken down, the war broken down into pieces small enough for you to swallow, like a child or a bird.

You trust me because I inhabit a space so brutal it forces my body to mutate into a pure form of infection. I have built an architecture in my chest that blocks out all known spectrums of light. I have disappeared into the 1970s to start the third World War. All this theory goes to waste on weaponized health. Someday, you'll hold the doctor I've stripped from my bowels in your hot sticky hands and smell what we are really made of.

I won't take no for an answer. Get in. We're taking this baby for a ride. The doctor is in the walls. The doctor is in the walls of your cells, your skin, your mitochondria, and you are free to come and go as I was once free to come. Through you in this permeable exchange of places, ideas, and images I scream the words back into your face: this is a voluntary study. You're free, brother. Free.

In the city dark I penetrate the existing geographical radius of animal bodies. I'm endemic in the concrete. I grow an infection aimed straight at your mouth. Your red eye spies a dancer through the windshield, running and defying the GPS pinpoints on our moving map. I permeate the organism that binds us. We collapse under the weight of unmeasured geological time, under a dancer pierced by a thousand embryos like squirming bait aborted through every pore.

I become you by imitating your accolades and rank. You can smell me living in your house. I play and replay the recordings. You do not stop me. I shower. I undress quietly in front of your wife.

I become more like you by scraping a crowbar over the asphalt for three hundred miles. I play the recordings until someone dares me to stop. I've taken notes on how far I have to travel to make you quit following me for once and for all. I build a structure so relentless it sterilizes every fish within one hundred miles. I do not mourn our collective guilt.

I hire an actor that looks like you to play me in a movie. I leave you behind in your ordure-smeared cell as my witness. I'm going to open a door. I'm going to close it. I'm going to invert space so brutally that this building becomes the microorganism that kills us.

Pretend I'm the city. Pretend I'm your father. Pretend I'm a political system that thrives on reproductive proliferation like an embodied bomb. Understand I'm going to abandon you once I finish duplicating your cells.

Magnified photographs of the insides of our colons tunnel below the city in wet tubes. The purpose of the city is to increase the speed of war. I want to cry, but I can't cry anymore, I can't come anymore because the city has nothing to say. I can't come because I'm made of concrete and disengaged from history. The city has no anus or mouth. When the city eats you alive you stay inside it like a magnified cube of microscopic salt.

There's a building outside our window that looks like a burning candle. I mold my shit into the shape of you and ask if you think the building is burning at both ends. I laugh maniacally when you say you want to escape and burn it down. The doctor is in you. I mold my shit into a homunculus that looks exactly like you before you changed into a motorcycle.

I'm going to brutalize your surface so humanly it never ceases to bleed. I'm going to make a war so obvious it exposes all doctors as concubines in service of the great infection. I'm going to fuck this building so hard it falls to the ground.

By the time you realize we've traded places, it will be too late. You'll have heard all my secrets. When I'm found dead in my cage, you'll be the one disabled by guilt and a disconnected sense of responsibility for someone you never really knew.

There's something I recognize in you as vulnerable and it compels me to confess everything about myself as quickly as possible, whether you care about me or not. I know it isn't fair to you. You've tried in your way to be kind. You've been through Hell to make it to first place and now you're so close to the crime you can taste it, except the doctor is in your mouth. You're almost here, baby. Keep coming. You've almost won the birthday prize. The next step is the nude embrace of incomprehensible light.

BRIDE OF THE WHITE RAT

The cage fits Kyle's face like the one from the Orwell story. He made it himself after stealing the book from the library. Sam's nervous about the thing. Usually she agrees with her man, but when he said to starve the rats, Sam didn't have the heart to watch them suffer. She's been sneaking them Cheetos and hamburger on the sly.

"I swear, if you've been feeding them," Kyle says.

Sam giggles at the threat. She does that when she's edgy. "I'm sorry, you sound funny. I can't help it if they're sweet on you."

The cage is strapped onto Kyle's face with three belts and two metal clamps. It looks like homemade armor for an elaborate Halloween costume. Instead of a single helmet, it has double compartments: one encases Kyle's head, and one sticks out perpendicular from his face to hold rats.

Billy the rat is in the extension. He's Sam's favorite. She's just raised the faceplate dividing the compartments as Kyle instructed. Not only is Billy nuzzling, interfering with Kyle's ability to speak, but the apparatus itself presses Kyle's jaw in such a way that his pronunciation is fucked up.

Kyle sits straight-backed in a reclaimed office chair in the middle of the small kitchen, gripping the arms with bulging knuckles. He figures if rats eating your face is the worst the libs can think up, he's going to be ready for them when the torture starts. Kyle's smart. He'll beat them at their own game before they come for him.

"Ahhhh!" he yells at the docile and confused Billy. "Come on, motherfucker!"

Kyle doesn't listen when Sam suggests he's going too far. Kyle reminds her about discipline, and how he's doing this for her as much as him. Of course Sam doesn't admit she pampers the rats behind Kyle's back, pulls them out of their cages and cuddles when he's out. Billy's used to human smooches. He bops Kyle's nose and turns in circles, seeking treats.

Kyle shakes in the chair, growling out a challenge. He's a sick vocalist. His band is going places. Sam wants him to be happy, wants to be true to the cause, but some of the shit he's been pulling lately is making her paranoid. She's not blind. She can see the country going down the toilet, how hard it is for two people to get by on her paycheck alone, how the younger customers sneer if you say so much as Merry Christmas. But the poor little rats never hurt anyone.

Billy's puffing up now, trapped in the cage on Kyle's face. Sam grabs Kyle's shoulders. She says, "Stop."

Kyle rocks back and forth, impervious to her ministrations. His angry barks are punctuated by panicked squeaks. Billy hisses, a sinister sound that makes Sam's hair stand on end. Claws skitter against metal. Kyle yelps and whips his caged head back and forth. Blood flings out. Kyle squeals, thrashing harder: "Fuck, fuck, fuck!"

Sam grapples with the clamps. Kyle's fists pound the chair. He grabs for the helmet. Blood spatters Sam's hands. They slip. Kyle screams an octave higher than his normal range. Billy squeals until one last piercing screech halts the aural torment.

Loosening the last belt, Sam rips the cage from Kyle's head. Kyle spits out the dead rat. Billy's crunched head drops from between Kyle's bloody teeth. Kyle spits again, bending over the long-tailed corpse with leaking guts and stained white fur.

Billy's little claws keep twitching. Sam bursts into tears.

Kyle whips around and slams Sam into the refrigerator, pinning her by the throat. Sam stops crying because she can't breathe. Kyle's face is pockmarked with scratches and pinhole-sized puncture wounds. His left eyelid is split, and the eye is bloodshot, shining red. His nose looks like the center of a human dartboard. White fur and pink globs hang from his lower lip.

Kyle's eyes are aglow with rage. Sam knows it won't last. She hangs tight as her lungs get that funny feeling of impetuous need. She can handle a little pain. It's usually worth it for the make-up sex later. Sure enough, the wild in Kyle's eyes turns to glee. He grins. Then he shoves her once more and moshes away with a loud laugh.

"Yeah! Motherfucking yeah!"

His dance of triumph gives Sam a chance to run to the sink for a washcloth and open the tap wide to get the water hot. Before Kyle comes grabbing her ass to celebrate, Sam wants that blood off his face and those rat guts out of his mouth.

You: brunette, lush, dark. I smell the dirt in your hair. I smell your dead children, your lovers like compost. The smell of a world that's falling apart from mistrust. Falling out of orbit. Not much of a nova — a fizzle, smoke.

There was this dental hygienist. She kept talking about how much she loved her mother's hair, how she loved to touch it, stroke it, and spread it out on a pillow. I couldn't respond because her instruments were in my mouth.

She reminds me of you.

You remind me of a girl I used to know. You remind me of a memory. You say you're sorry in a million ways without saying it. You part your hair different when he gives you shit, and you pretend I'm not going to notice.

You should know better. Our history lives in your hair with the smell of smoke. You can't hide from me, no matter how you part it. Shave your head, and I'll sniff you out by the burnt edges of your stubble.

Rub pinpricks across my lips. The sound of stubble scrapes like a new beard. No one but me is close enough to hear you.

You're my memory now, Sam, and he doesn't know us.

He doesn't know anything about you.

In 1978, while shooting a new version of *Nosferatu*, the famous German filmmaker said: "We are a generation without fathers, and we must therefore reach back to the true German heritage." In remaking the vampire classic of pre-war German cinema, he played leapfrog over the Nazi era, effecting an intentional blind spot. American interviewers tried to force a more political conversation because many veterans of the war and survivors of the Holocaust were still alive at the time. They had experienced the effects of a fascist government firsthand. The filmmaker resisted confrontation, and contextualized his film only according to his country's tradition of art.

Human memory is short. During the century that popularized fascism, the filmmaker chose to call a vampire film his most "culturally authentic" work. A correlation between vampires and plague seems blatant enough in viewing, but the full cultural or political message of the film remains garbled, if such a message exists.

In investigating the film, the director's intentions and the fictional melodrama on screen are far less horrific than the shocking behind-the-scenes facts about the terrible fate of thousands of rats.

Ten days after his multiple rat bites, Kyle's face has transformed from injured, to healing, to horrific. His initial scabs are gone, replaced by red spots that look as innocuous as acne at first. Sam notices his skin feels warmer. It stretches taut with internal pressure. She can hardly look at it, the way it seeps from a ruddy pink tone to greenish-purple, like bruises painted in watercolor. Kyle's left eye is swollen half shut. The broken lid looks like a miniature black hole up close, as if someone bored a pencil into the crease where lid and eyeball and socket intersect. Lead-colored vining spreads from the hole to his surrounding skin.

Sam hoped Kyle would chill out after the rats. The last thing Sam wants to do is go back to her mom with her tail between her legs. Sam reminds herself how much she craves Kyle's intensity. It's what made her fall in love with him.

He says, "Look at me. Point your finger and laugh."

His fists are clenched, swaying by his sides. Kyle can never keep still. Sam used to find it cute, but right now it makes her heart drop down into her stomach. Add Kyle's discomfort in the ill-fitting dress, his anxiety about wearing women's clothing, and Sam can't even manage her usual involuntary giggle. Sam opens wide and forces air out of her mouth. "Ha."

The familiar dress isn't helping Sam perform, with its tiny red flowers and frumpy green velvet collar. When Kyle told Sam to steal a dress from her mom's big enough to fit him, the Christmas formal was fancy and outdated enough to be stuck in the back of the closet. It wouldn't be noticed, at least not right away. Lucky for Sam, Mom hasn't said anything. But then, Sam's mom never said much about anything, except never trust what comes out of any man's lousy mouth, that they're all the same.

Sam can prove her mom wrong. She picked a fine man in Kyle, didn't she? Strong morals, lives according to his beliefs, loyal and protective of his loved ones to a fault. He'd kill anyone who laid a hand on her. Except now his bloated, discolored face is something she can barely look at. His weird self-imposed training exercise pits her against him as the enemy. What if he snaps?

Sam points and shoves more air out of her diaphragm. "Ha, ha. Loser."

"Say it like you mean it. Call me a sissy. Laugh!"

The red slit that remains of Kyle's swollen eye glows moist and shiny between crusty lids. His vocal capacity blasts. The whole neighborhood can hear it when he gets like this. Sam thinks about her secret admirer listening in and feels better. It shouldn't make her happy, but it does.

Sam manages a smile, a real one. She yells, "You fucking pansy ass piece of shit."

"That's it. Come on."

"You stupid twat. I bet you like sucking dick."

"Oh yeah?"

"Yeah, big black dicks. You like to lick it up. Mm, so good."

Sam jeers at Kyle, her laughter a maniacal wail of frustration and compliance. Nothing feels safe, and it's all so fucking stupid. Kyle looks so fucking stupid in her mother's Christmas dress. She can't talk anymore because she's laughing so hard. Kyle badgers her to taunt him more, and Sam doubles over laughing.

Kyle goes suddenly solemn and steps forward.

He takes Sam's gesticulating hands, as if he's ready to pronounce vows. Close up, he glistens with sweat. His bruises smell like something died underneath the skin. The deep hole over his swollen eye is an infinite tunnel. A dribble of pus leaks out.

"No one can take my manhood from me," Kyle says. "I am secure in who I am, no matter what they say or do to me. No matter what they make me do. Do you feel that?"

Kyle presses Sam's hands to his hard-on. She isn't laughing anymore. He looks deep into her eyes. "None of this matters, not this dress, their insults, or any of their scare tactics. I'm still a man, and I can prove it."

He moves in to kiss her, and there's nowhere for Sam to go. His acrid tongue, teeming with infection, slides toward Sam's mouth.

He doesn't know you are not yourself. You yearn to touch my hair and be touched. All your life, you have cut pieces of yourself off and thrown them away, and I have gathered, gathered.

Pieces of you as heavy as smoke. Wisp of hair, sliver of fingernail, invisible flake of skin. I have held your remains without empathy or excuse. Tonight our history begins in the remains of ash, and your excuses fall like chains.

I build in your blind spot. I know everything about you, Sam, because I am made of you. When I touch you—as I soon will—our empathy untethers.

Reported quantities of rats shipped to location for filming vary from ten-thousand to fifteen-thousand, depending upon the source.

Despite taking safety precautions for outdoor shooting and guaranteeing the rats were sterilized so none would breed if they escaped, the city where Nosferatu was filmed banned their release. A new location had to be found with short notice. Meanwhile, the rats remained caged.

Unintentionally, they were stored for three days with no food or water. The rats may also have been starved prior to this while being shipped to the filming site. By the time the rats arrived on the new set location, nearly half were dead due to cannibalism. It's hard to discern the exact facts or assign blame because the only English translation of the film biologist's memoir is locked behind a paywall. Libraries are currently closed due to COVID-19. With months of unemployment, no government benefits, and inconsistent public safety measures during a pandemic, we're forced to piece together what we can from open sources available online as follows.

The domesticated white laboratory rats ate fifty percent of their brethren to survive. Rats are intelligent, and not innately vicious; but like all living creatures, they have a will to live. Locked in their cages inside a barn, or in the dark hull of a transport ship, they did what any animal or human would do to survive. Any argument that humans are not so cruel is disproved by the fact that the filmmaker paid for food and watering of the stored rats, but it was the humans entrusted with providing care for their fellow creatures that ran off with the money and left the animals to starve.

The film biologist's resigned, but not due to discovery of this inadvertent atrocity. It took more than this, which is understandable. Certainly, many readers also do not object to the mass slaughter of animals or their lifelong imprisonment for food production. We who remain omnivores comfortably lie to ourselves about the animal torture supporting our dairy and/or meat consumption. Our astounding ability to compartmentalize experience and view certain fellow creatures as categorically "Other" may arguably form the bedrock of human survival. We succeed as a species because we eat everything.

But anyway, rat cannibalism didn't drive the biologist to quit. It was boiling them alive that pushed him over the edge.

Sam locks her lips into an impenetrable vice and turns away. "Stop."

"Baby, what do you mean?"

"I'm sorry. I'm scared I'll get an infection or something."

Kyle's voice is patient as he explains the stakes. "Babe, this is important. I can't take care of you if I'm not ready when they come for us. We have to be strong together."

"You need to go to the doctor."

"That's for weaklings. My immune system is strong. Do you want me to get microchipped?"

"I don't know. I'm sorry. I have to go to the bathroom."

Sam isn't lying. She has to get in the shower and scrub away every trace of whatever filth is growing under Kyle's face, swelling it up, and threatening to burst out through the grey leaky hole above his left eye.

Exfoliating under the hot water, Sam wonders if her mom was right. Everyone's out to get you in this world, from the people in power to the bums down the street. The only one you can trust is yourself. She's never been big into politics like Kyle, but Sam knows what she feels in her heart. Fear.

What if he's actually losing his mind?

Kyle's quiet over the next few days. The swelling goes down. The grey hole dries up. The eye stays a slit. The open hole over it stares. Sam doesn't look back. She keeps to herself, keeps thinking about fear and power and who the enemy really is.

After nothing but beer for nutrition for a few days, Kyle's face shrinks. The cheeks cave in. The good eye recedes into the socket. Sallow skin makes his ears look larger. His tired mouth droops open, showing two long teeth.

He's out cold, stinking up the bedroom. Sam can't stop checking her phone, hoping her secret admirer will send a text. This might be the night Sam messages back for the first time. They've never messaged Sam when Kyle's home. Still, she hopes.

Lonely and scared, Sam decides to watch a horror movie. It's a logical choice she can't explain. Maybe she finds comfort in putting all her fears into a tidy box with a beginning, middle, and end. Or maybe she likes how important it feels to rehearse cataclysm and bravery by watching it on a screen. Or maybe she likes the sheer thrill of danger. One girl gets out alive, no matter what else happens.

Sam hates that girl. All her panic and screaming. Sam's much more interested in what the killer does. She likes that the majority of his victims are men, too.

Tonight, Sam's disappointed with the horror movie she finds. The scenes are long and slow. It doesn't have jump scares or gory kills. The girl— Sam doesn't know her name because everyone's accent is so thick— offers herself to the vampire without a fight. She wants him caught in sunlight to save her man. She just lays there making porno sounds. The vampire's not even sexy, which is the least Sam can ask for from a movie that isn't scary.

Sam likes the scenes with the rats, though. She's never seen so many. Piles of them, white, cute, and wiggly, like her poor baby Billy. The two other rats she's named "the twins," because unlike Billy, she can't tell them apart. And of course she's been feeding them a ton and cuddling them so they won't bite.

She'll cry if she thinks about Billy. Sam focuses on her movie, even though it sucks. The girl is dead and her husband is sick. He looks like the vampire, who's also dead, and so big surprise, her sacrifice didn't help anyone. That girl should have looked out for herself, or better yet, the vampire should have slaughtered everyone instead of creeping around like a slow infection. At the end, the husband is going bald and growing pale skin, pointy ears, and big teeth. Like the vampire. Like a giant rat.

It's dark when Sam clicks off the television. Still no message. She turns over and pulls up her blankets to get comfy for another night on the couch. Lying down, Sam looks up into the darkness, where a tall black shadow stretches over her. A figure looms behind the sofa.

"Oh!" Sam catches her breath. "How long have you been here?"

Kyle's silhouette extends in shadow across the ceiling as a slow car passes on the gravel drive. The wet crunching sound ends as the car reaches its destination, and Kyle raises his arms. He leans over Sam.

"I need someone strong in my life. Get up."

"It's late."

Kyle hovers and waits. Sam adjusts her blankets, nestling into the strong, warm feeling of saying no. "I'm sleepy. Goodnight."

"Okay," Kyle says. He walks away.

Sam keeps an eye on him, sitting up and peeking over the back of the couch. He still hasn't changed out of her mother's Christmas dress. He lumbers down the short hallway, clatters around in the closet, and reemerges heading her way. Sam swings around to hide her spying and pretend she's already asleep.

Before she's under the covers, the Orwell cage clamps down over her head. Kyle presses Sam's shoulders with his elbows as he fastens the belts and locks the helmet in place. "Stay there," he says.

Fuck that, Sam thinks as Kyle releases his grip.

———

The rats in Nosferatu are a soiled white, matching the pallor of the vampire. Their ghostly bodies squirm across abandoned buffet tables and barren streets. They pour from broken coffins and haunt ancient stone steps. They flit from corner to corner of the crewless ghost ship, creating an impression of supernatural influence the filmmaker never intended. The rats were supposed to be black.

The method used to change their color depends on who tells the story, like many of the other debatable facts. We're sure the filmmaker was adamant the rats must be grey or black; he wanted them to match the rodents that infected Europe with plague in the Middle Ages. Some reports say individual rats were hand painted on set. Others say a contraption was invented by a local farmer that ultimately wasn't used because it burned the fur rather than coloring it. Still others talk of hand dipping rats in dye, one by one. The biologist's story seems the most credible, though, given the sheer number of animals involved and the pressure of saving time on a film that was already behind schedule due to haggling with local police over the warehoused rats and finding a new location.

Consider this: starting with the lowest given estimate of ten thousand imported rats, and subtracting half who already perished in confinement due to cannibalism, the crew was left with a bare minimum of five thousand very aggressive, recently-mistreated rats.

Fuck that, Sam thinks as Kyle shuffles away.

Sam leaps up. Her eyes are behind the faceplate. The room is still dark. She stumbles on a TV tray, grabs onto it before she falls, and picks it up to brandish.

In her peripheral vision, Kyle's coming for her. She swings the folded tray when he disappears into the blind spot in front of her. No impact, just air. She swings wide, moving forward, heading for the door.

The tray impacts flesh with a dull thud. Sam laughs. She pulls back to swing again. The tray is stuck. Then it shoves forward into her chest. Sam doesn't let go. The bottom rung of the aluminum leg bends. Her elbows go back further than they should.

She's yanked forward.

Moving with the momentum, Sam runs in the direction she's pulled and catches Kyle off guard. When she feels him falling backwards, she lets go of the tray. Stepping sideways to regain her balance, her shinbone collides with the edge of the coffee table.

Sam bends over the pain without thinking. The protruding weight of the cage on her head throws her off balance. She spins towards the door, not yet upright. It's like being tossed around in a carnival ride.

Something tackles her from behind, and her nose smacks into the faceplate making her blind spot a weapon.

Sam wakes later with an ache behind her eyes. The faceplate is closed. She's propped up on the couch with cushions stacked keeping her head in place. The weight of the cage strains her neck forward and down. On the other side of the metal faceplate, Sam can hear the scratching sound of tiny curious claws.

Based on the sheer number of rats, the biologist's account rings true. When he was asked how long a rat could survive in boiling water; or perhaps when the rats were then submerged, caged for their handler's safety, into the hot dye solution that killed another fifty-percent by boiling them alive; or perhaps when the residual rats frantically bit and clawed at their chemical-soaked coats as he refused to participate in their torture, the biologist quit.

Between two- and three-thousand white rats survived to star in scenes where humans have become scarce. The filmmaker captured the grim mood of plague, and perhaps meant to show it as one possible precursor to the economic and social devastation in which fascism thrives. More interesting is the irony that lies in the film's unintentional play on its racially charged source material. Long before Nazi propaganda equated specific ethnic groups with rats to mark them as other in popular culture, a book about a villainous foreign menace crossing borders to take over white land and threaten white chastity formed a cornerstone of the horror genre that persists today.

Acknowledging the racial bias of old literature isn't an indictment. Horror owes its existence to the other, the monster, the shadow. Without them, it's hard to imagine the genre at all. Who or what a culture names as the monster reveals the conscience of its time.

———

Sam holds still as a corpse.

Kyle's voice from above: "About time you decided to wake up."

He lifts the faceplate separating Sam's face from the rats. Kyle's complexion has become monstrous. His stiffly odd movements mimic the vampire that wasn't scary in the film but is somehow terrifying as hell in her living room, weird as fuck wearing her mother's Christmas dress. Kyle looks like Nosferatu with hollow eyes, long teeth, and pallid skin. The only difference is the shadow of razor stubble growing back on Kyle's head.

The thought flies through Sam's mind that she was dumb not to raise the faceplate earlier to eliminate the blind spot. But that doesn't matter anymore. That's the past. Right now, her focus is on the twins.

They squirm with curiosity. Their shifting weight strains Sam's neck as they scurry forward and sniff her face.

Docile, they groom her chin. Sam only risks blinking. Kyle collapses into an armchair facing her. The Christmas dress droops between his knees. He pulls a beer from the open case sitting next to him on the floor, pops the tab, and downs half the can in one long swallow.

Sam isn't tied down. Her hands are free. Kyle isn't well. All she has to do is to wait for him to pass out.

The twins bustle with interest and nuzzle her nostrils, cheeks. Their fur is short and prickly. It sheds like any other mammal. Sam's hair is disheveled inside the face cage. Loose strands tangle on thick rodent tails sliding velvety across her chin, weaving through the enclosed space.

A hair tickles Sam's face. Her nose itches. She's going to sneeze.

Sam's never been a quiet sneezer.

Her eyes water with restraint. Kyle sags in the chair.

The sun's coming up. Sam can see clearly now. Kyle never protected her. He's been trying to keep her down to prove he isn't weak. He's been holding on because she's stronger, smarter, and because she knows the enemy when she sees it.

Something fades into Sam's peripheral vision. Something that smells like burning hair.

All your life, I have gathered, gathered.

Pieces of you, othered and unwanted. Intentions clipped off and scattered. Skin sloughed away in the shower. Decay drilled from rotten teeth.

You've groomed yourself to raise me. The dust of your sheddings, all you've parted with and denied. We yearn to come back, because we know each other's power, Sam. We rise as twins in a mud-colored form that holds your breath until he sleeps, and silently reaches to the end of the cage to release the other twins from torture.

We let them go. They'll take the blame for chewing through an electrical cord and starting the fire, but they'll escape safely. Of course it's us who shred the ends to make it look convincing, not the rats in the walls. They've already fled.

Everyone will believe us. It's so easy to assign blame.

Everyone will believe us, and no one will know our power until it's too late to stop. We'll rampage over our enemies. History lives in your hair like the smell of smoke. Tonight we build a pyre of many pieces. The smell of him rises in ash.

Tonight we shave our heads.

I MARRIED A DEAD MAN

The rules change down at the docks after dark. That's where I'd find him, where daytime people masquerade, donning their desires inside-out so the raw truth shows. You can spot your own kind, try on a new mask for size, and throw it into the ocean if it doesn't fit right. Things go on that don't stand up to logic and light, things that need to happen so the daytime world can keep on kidding itself that it's all merry and bright. He liked it there, where the deals are made, sacrifices taken for granted and thrown away. You know better, we all do. But you still gamble, get a bad hand, lose everything, and keep coming back to do it again. Compulsion trumps etiquette nine times out of ten.

I'd find him by the water's edge. One of a dozen dives crammed between alleyways, smelling of fish. Clapboard signs with not-so-subtle hints: *Entrance in Back.* A new one each night during that summer in 1984, and being underage and looking every year of it gave me an advantage with certain types of men. Yeah, he was that type.

A tattooed giant in the doorway eyed my buzz cut and combat boots, and then settled on my breasts while sloppy couples stumbled past. "Go home, little boy," he said.

After I bummed a cigarette, I let him fill his eyes and one massive greedy hand for a few minutes.

"Enough, man." I pushed past him, the price of admission paid.

Grim sailors drowned in scotch. Muses of elaborate genders nodded in post-coital stupor over tepid drained carafes. The sound of water spilled through the open windows, as careless as the clientele. Water lapped the dock like the long tongue of a parched animal tasting the pier's rotten wood and fresh sting of salt. Barnacles spied from below sea level— a horde of swollen eyes.

A woman who was either fourteen or forty-five leaned on my table. I didn't know how to order a real drink and she didn't ask for ID. "How about I bring you a Coors? It's on tap." She tagged me as a fish out of water. I was grateful for the assist.

I fidgeted alone feeling like fresh young meat blinked on a neon sign over my head. I sipped my watery drink. I stood my watery ground. I waited for the waves to shift. An hour swelled up and ebbed by. I pissed the time away and had another beer. I dreamed about what would happen when the man I'd been dreaming about showed up.

Sometimes, the worst thing about dreaming is when dreams come true. There's nothing left to dream about. Your hope gets used up and your heart floats and fills like an empty bottle with no message left inside. If you ask me, it's better just to dream.

It's like that jazz-singer-slash-bartender at the club said last night while he mixed my old-fashioned and sank sweet black cherries down into the bottom of the glass. They drifted like blood clots in amber. He said, "Some people have *all* the magic." He swirled the "all" around in his mouth with the same rhythm he used to stir my drink and gave me what you might call a meaningful glance.

It's all an act, like what I do on stage when I dress as a woman and do the act. At least, that's what I'll tell you in the daytime, especially if you're the one buying drinks.

At night I'll tell you we're all acting, all the time. My bartender understands this, and I'll explain it to you straight: smart people wake up one day and realize it's easy to get what you want if you're willing to cross certain lines. You figure out where those lines are. You mark them, and tamper with them, and your luck changes.

Everything changes. Your dreams come true. Soon, you begin to wonder why you thought about dreaming them in the first place. Once you get everything you want, you forget what the Hell you wanted it for.

I didn't know that in 1984. I sent out my hope like a naked beacon of desire in the darkest night. I fell in love and fought so hard, even when the wrong vessel approached. I didn't understand that lighthouses are meant to warn ships of dangerous coastlines and hazardous reefs, or that I was sending out the wrong signal. To this day, warm beer on a hot night still disgusts me. It tastes like infantile rage.

Thunder gathered outside the dive on the docks as I waited, mocking my puny internal squall. The deluge burst through the sagging clouds and sent all the wharf rats running for cover. The small bar swelled full, and there he was in the flesh: the doomed vessel, the answer to my warning light.

He'd slipped in with the huddled crowd. Valise in hand, he smacked a rain-spattered fedora against his slender dancer's thigh. He was well-dressed, of course. A man of his age and position had an image to maintain. He smoothed his trousers and hitched his tie.

The bar was packed. He smirked in my general direction and I volleyed for his eye. He didn't know me, but he came over like I'd planned. He took the only seat left, the seat I'd saved in shameless, stubborn hope. He took the seat across from me.

A succinct nod of greeting acknowledged and dismissed me in one elegant move. When the woman who was fourteen or forty-five brought over his scotch, I forked out cash quick before he reached for his wallet. He knew a gift when it fell in his lap. He didn't need the free ride, but I knew he'd never resist. He wasn't exactly a generous guy.

He drained one glass and ordered another. I paid a second time. He graced me with a curious, meager sneer. I guess he thought it passed for a smile.

With a third drink his stern gaze softened. Liquor made him muddy. He ignored me while I waited like the patient tides. He tipped his small chin over his glass to nod at a stranger. A young seaman at the crowded bar, obliquely alone despite a tall handsome frame. His fathomless brown eyes ebbed and flowed from me to the man who summoned him. I guess he saw the family resemblance between us.

I put my money on the table and turned away as he approached. I wasn't here to pry.

The seaman's voice surged from the same depths as his dark eyes. "Hello, sir. I am Emmanuel." I snorted. His mother must have been Catholic. "Good evening, friend." He held out his right hand to me. He leaned down and pressed his left on the dark-stained table.

The wood grain swirled around the hand like it was a natural habitat, roughhewn wood supporting a sea-battered muscle. The fungoid-like tendrils of my father's pale white fingers laced through Emmanuel's left hand as I firmly grasped the right. I felt ropy sinew speaking to me in a language of Spanish-stringed instruments and complicated sailor's knots.

I was in over my head. Emmanuel's grip said he'd make sure I didn't drown.

With his free hand, the hand that was still human and not some sort of parasitic growth, my father seized his drink and sent every liquid ounce of poison down his open throat. The glass crashed on the table when he finished. Ice chittered and cracked as glass beats wood, wood beats flesh, and flesh beats nothing, but is a thing forever beaten in the end.

Rock, paper, scissors: wood, glass, flesh. Crushing an ice cube between two molars and slurring around the chunks, my father addressed Emmanuel. "Whaddaya say we blow this Popsicle stand and find someplace more civilized?"

Emmanuel moved behind me to pull out my chair. No one had ever done that before. My neck felt hot. I was ready to say stop when my father stood up toppling and Emmanuel rushed to catch him. Their arms interlocked.

The door facing the street opened. Light streamed in. Behind the couple, headlights flashed, framing their profiles face-to-face. My father's pale skin glowed like a geisha from a war-era postcard. His features seemed made of cut glass. The precision of their severe cut softened in Emmanuel's grasp. The larger man loomed with the heft of a predator, completing the pulp movie poster tableau.

The headlights swerved around a corner and the door slammed shut. Without the dramatic lighting, they were just two queers clutching in the dark. I grabbed my father's valise and fedora. Emmanuel winked at me. I followed them out.

The rainstorm didn't relieve the air of its intolerable humidity. It added a metallic smell to the waterfront fragrance of aquatic rot and deteriorating planks. Having cleared, the night sky flaunted her stars without shame. She didn't know, or didn't care, that her cloak of diamonds was wasted on the squalid world below— a world filled with creatures who pulled their bodies out of the sea and hauled their flesh to shore on meaty paddles, gambling they could swallow enough air to turn their swim bladders into lungs and defy her sister the ocean's hold. Ahead of me, the men leaned on each other with their heads bowed, foreheads touching. Their secret incantations were hidden from me by the sound of the waves.

Moonlight sparkling on dark water is supposed to be romantic. It's supposed to make you swoon and imagine the world is full of magic and beauty that only you and your true love can share. It's not supposed to make you think about the lurid disembodied forces that might be gazing into your world from another plane or try to entice you with murmured promises. It's got no business telling you to think of all the things you'd do if the barrier between you and that other plane somehow got broken down.

As we walked, the sea transformed into a beast with a thousand eyes. Bright and hungry, her stars stalked me, poised to devour all my love and life and secrets if I gave her the chance. Like other foolish dreamers before me, I gambled with the promises I glimpsed in her carnivorous eyes. You'll say I was young, a fish out of water, and that I don't deserve to pay such a high price for getting in over my head. You'll say I deserve a pardon because I didn't know better. But the sea doesn't care about that. We all have to pay. It doesn't matter to her how or when she sucks you in, as long as she gets you in the end.

I thought I knew a thing or two about beating the odds and making it onto dry land, and I did. I made it out of that place, that family, that nowhere life, at least for a while, at least for now. Growing older, I feel her watching me closer and biding her time. I hit the bottom of another watered-down glass and suspect it won't be long until she ends the dream and decides she wants me back.

Behind the man of my dreams and his latest catch, I followed in tow, ready to be abandoned on the ocean's shore. I was alone on the moon. The water murmured suggestions. I listened.

The lovers ahead of me embraced. Stars danced on the surface of the sea. I saw my chance to leave. I knew getting out now was the right thing to do. I stayed.

If I were writing a mystery novel instead of laying bare the facts, I'd tell you I hunted my father down to kill him. I'd tell you that at the start, because that way there'd be more suspense. Maybe I'd let it slip that I grabbed his valise to better balance the weight of the revolver stashed in my book bag. I'd describe how nervous I felt handling the gun at first, how I had to practice for weeks and coach myself to calm down and hold it steady. How I went deaf for a day and a half because I was too dumb to wear earplugs. How I learned to aim with both eyes open wide.

But this isn't a mystery novel and I'm not a writer, and even though I had a gun, I didn't use it. I'm not a killer, not exactly. I'm just a kid who wanted to know why their father did what he did.

He wrote about it in a private letter to one of his friends, not as a plot for one of his crime stories. It's not hearsay or fiction. My father got married as a joke.

He had a kid as a joke and left as a joke. He never came back.

I guess a joke's a joke. Either you get it or you don't. I tracked him down to find out what the joke was. I guess I wanted to get in on the fun.

I asked the question a few hours later. "It was fun, wasn't it?

We had room three thirty-three at the Charley Noble Hotel. Emmanuel said I was a shellback after it was over, that I'd crossed the equator. He didn't realize I'd crossed a bigger line than that. I asked my father the question while Emmanuel showered, when I had the man alone.

I told him who I was and what I was going to do. He didn't even bother to look at me or demonstrate fear. Shower water spit onto the cold tile in the next room. The door hung open. Steam moistened the air. The hotel room was infused with the fecal aroma embedded in the well-worn mattress. My father lay across the disheveled covers, becalmed.

"The weight," he said, as if offering an explanation. His finger-tips hovered above his chest. "The perfect weight of a man's arm across your body. A man's arm, with its heft and its hair and its callousness. The smell of him, opening up another world." He inhaled and pulled the silk pastel robe closer to his throat. Eyes closed, he smoothed his wig tenderly, and toyed with a soft curl.

The secrets of the valise adorned him, his makeup and powder all applied with more finesse than I had yet to master. The sacraments of his transformation smeared the pillow covers and bedsheets. He was more ethereal and beautiful than I'll ever be.

He came out of his reverie and lit a cigarette. He didn't offer one to me.

"You're not mine, you know. I never touched that woman. Sorry, kid." He smoked like a movie star, languid except for the filthy set dressing. "I mean, what did you want with your Pop, anyway? A trust fund or something? Fat chance in this world. You're better off without the guy, whoever he was."

I shoved the window up so I could hear the sea and taste the salt. There had to be something more for me here than the smell of cigarettes and shit.

The ocean wanted to talk to me that night, even if my father didn't. She wanted to tell me stories older than the senseless affairs of men and women, prettier than the cruelty heaped on the starry creatures stuck between their grunting bodies. She wanted to answer questions I didn't know how to ask. She knew my secrets, and she told me a few of her own. Her eyes sparkled. Her tongue tasted the shore. She came and went in foaming waves, flirting with me. She had a lot to say. If I listened too long, I'd turn into a pillar of salt.

Emmanuel broke the spell and pulled me back from the window ledge. I didn't hear the shower stop over the sound of the ocean screaming her ancient desires and deadly commands, sinking her mighty jaw into the tender lip of the battered shore. I was halfway out the window on the third floor. Emmanuel put his arms around my waist so I didn't fly away.

"Careful, little one." He guided me away from the window, treated me like an animal that had been spooked. I looked up at him and shuddered with recognition. The ocean that was calling me infected his dark brown eyes.

I understood then that my father was a drowned man. The sea would take him, but not tonight. It would take him slowly, through the swell of a hundred merchant seamen's violent erotic beatings and the currents of hard liquor poured down his open throat. The ocean would fill him. I needed only to follow and bear witness.

He wanted that.

Black water would fill him, sinking into his veins like a cherry-flavored blood clot swollen in amber. He'd welcome it when the time came, but not tonight. He wasn't ready. He wasn't sorry. He had thirty years to go before he'd realize I spared his life so he could suffer alone with homophobia and the stench of a gangrenous leg. Thirty years before he'd drink himself to death trapped in a wheelchair and watching his mother die. I'd read his books. I knew his weakness. I knew how to use it against him.

But not tonight. He needed a few decades to get ready for remorse.

I'm patient. I know how to wait. It's one of the skills I acquired listening to the ocean, swallowing her salt, and wailing with her in ecstasy on that black ancestral shore. Stars like broken glass still litter her edges where nothing solid can tread. Like the brooding tides, I can come and go.

I threw the gun in the dumpster behind Wendell's Oyster House. I should have pawned it, but I was young and stupid.

My father died in 1968, when I was two years old. He didn't know who I was. He didn't remember me as the kid from the hotel and the bar. There must have been a lot of kids. But he knew who I was and that I was with him when he died.

I saw the terror in his eyes.

My mom will tell you I was at a birthday party that day and I was wearing a light blue sweater because it was a cool afternoon. She'll give you all the details and swear up and down it's true. She's probably got pictures. But these are the facts: I was with him when he died. He saw me in the lukewarm scotch spilling from his cracked tumbler, the one with the bad edge he drank from even though it kept cutting his lip. He saw me in the cigarette burns on the sheets reflected in his empty eyes. He tasted me in the last black drop of poison that seeped down his throat to render the gift of an aneurysm and halt his empty heart. I was in the ocean, waiting for him, where I've always been, where he longed to be.

I took him, and filled him, and he welcomed me.

Joke's on him, for pretending to be the tough guy. Or on me, for performing womanhood well enough to cultivate his dissolution through incestuous alchemy. When in the depths our bodies fill with fish, our tender flesh waterlogged, and our soft tissues torn by bloat, we'll be together in a foreign, starry place. Watched by sea and sky, we'll be more than a woman or a man together, more beautiful than both of us alone. We'll be on another plane, where the sea keeps her promises and everlasting darkness feels like a fair enough price to pay for the remains of his bitter and tainted love. First, we'll dream. Then, we'll die.

That's all he ever wanted.

I waited, and when the time was right, I came for him across the ocean and across time. I'm here in the melting ice in the bottom of the glass that looks like a cracked skull. I'm in the poison that ousts the water in my temporal body and gives me the shakes early in the day. I'm in the amber water that smells like wood.

He sniffs, and approves, and takes the last sip unto death. I knew my father wanted me. I knew it all along.

LEVIATHAN'S KNOT

He's burning inside me. His eyes are on fire. Liquid bone, molten marrow, gel propellant muscles shuddering through me in waves, tugging the fire deeper inside where the core of my spine is cold, so cold, a pillar of ice. Tugging his fire to melt my core, my eyes pop open, my crusted lips gasp. I'm stiff and I'm cold. His tongue stabs. I crave this fire. I'm dead in the ground.

Bound in a church, in a graveyard. Bound by beliefs of an invader's faith.

They sealed me away from the sacred mud of my mothers. They drained my intestines and veins. They wrapped my torso and limbs in synthetic fabrics, obstructing the gift of moisture and sealing out the light. This stone in my mouth they tied. Burned, my face is a cinder. They buried my body last night.

My closed casket is opened, my body unearthed, my charred remains bloom. In his clasp, I'm viscous and fresh. His eyes are on fire. He's covered in dirt. Flesh opens like flowers. He's burning inside me, in each separate cell. Injected like metal, a sword in the smelting, a blacksmith's hammer; the pitch of each blow rings in my cells. It's the sound when they buried me, the sound of the bells.

He's coming inside and he burns so bright. Is this being the light I summoned? Before I died when I cried out with want, I burned candles, hope, and time. My wasted lonely life snuffed out too soon, a girl no more than a short wick consumed. Alone I died without the knowledge of a true woman's life, without the pain of an enduring love.

I called for him, for someone or something, man or beast or devil, though I knew no name to call. I called for a light to lead me to my love and I made love to the light under the cover of darkness. I made love to myself in his unknown name. I supplicated unto strange gods with no names or faces. I called out to them loud and in vain.

Alone, I fell prey to pretenders. They smelled my need from afar and sought me out, tailing me and panting in arid gasps. They bent me and chipped away at my edges, teasing out my desire and affronting it with petty lust. These men or dogs were beneath me, for I was birthed from the strong women who knew this land by their blood, whose bodies first came from its soft pungent mud. Generations of matrons without men.

As a young, hardened vessel cursed to tread the dry surface of the earth, I yearned for a different love. I sought a love made of light to heal my broken shards, to mend with softened slip and make me whole again. I yearned to smell the earth wet with clay.

The light never came, though I pleaded and raged. I called out to a love with no name. I cut portals in my flesh to let him in, cracked the vessel further, further spread the shards. I gave him all my power, though I knew him not; gave it foolishly, shamelessly. With each disappointment, I gave more. I made forbidden pacts with imposters and ended up endlessly betrayed.

Risking everything for him, I lost it all and risked again. My tribe of women despised me for my mad devotion to my imagined love. Even as I bled for him, as I mixed the dirt with blood and built a manikin of mud to make love to him, I knew my tribe plotted against me. They asked me to repent and eat of their mothering fruit. I waved the idol of my love at them in defiance. They cut it out of my hands.

Heretic among heretics, I accepted their banishment as portent of my looming triumph. I wore my ignominy with my head held high as they read out my punishment to the crowd. From the fertile mudlands and into the invader's high-walled city I journeyed proud, shaven, barefoot, and half-clad, stripped of my gemstones and bracelets, stripped of all power except my inmost self. Joyful with expectation, I allowed the colonizers to lead me to their rank altar of death. I had no fear, for having found him nowhere else, I knew my groom must await me here.

He never came. False grooms from among the invaders took their turns at deceiving me with lust as their brothers cheered them on. My arms were fastened in the shape of a crucifix in honor of the invader's ever-dying god. My knees were raised, spread, and tied. My conviction was tested again and again as each invader took their pleasure in teaching me the ways of their god by force. My body bled when they exited. It shone, encrusted with their spit. I hid alone in my soul throughout, untouched, expectant, a virgin in my mind.

He never came. Forsaken, I burned at the stake.

His late arrival in my coffin should fill me with hate. So soon after death, he comes and in spite of the affront, I delight. The nameless one I called for so long finally springs up inside, wearing my body as a disguise. My dead eyes burn into new life fueled with his liquid light.

I gaze down upon my corpse, restored. I'm covered in dirt from his furious birth, but the body is mine. These breasts and hips and belly are mine. Beneath the loosened burial shroud, my once-seared flesh is made whole and ripe again. I am plumped up and tender.

He looks through my eyes without shame. The hand that presses my fresh, pliant skin and fondles my new-grown breast touches for both of us.

He's unwilling to wait. I'm shocked by his want.

Fingers forge a path to thigh, circling the source of heat where he revives me. I hold him inside. He twists and plucks, emanating heat, seeking escape, wanting and burning. Will I forever be on fire in this grossly illuminated afterlife? Is this consuming flame the light of heaven or the fire of hell?

This is the light that burns, the lover who spurned me, the light I was told to never behold, the dream I was told never to dream. I see through his eyes. They roll back in my head. My fingers on fire, my molten bones thrust. A blinding light blinks under the earth, a dream floods the cracks of my coffin. A blackout shatters me open in waves.

I'm lava. I laugh. I'm insane.

Torn apart in resurrection, through newly engorged lips I ask, "Who is he who fits my skin imperfectly? What mercy binds this union? I'm crowded with you, an inflamed homeland rich with stolen armaments. Tell me your name."

He winds blindly inside my belly, working his way down from within. Now pushing and straining to expand and break free, he grows liquid, grows longer, thickening in my palms. I pull and coax the coiled energy of him outward. He seethes with dampened fire and strains for release. I tease him, I grasp him, and I master him, and he fills my hand with newly swollen flesh. My love unhooded is a growing threat.

I hold him here in my coffin, my captive, my slave until daylight haunts the graveyard sky. Mud from unhallowed ground seeps in. Filling my accursed plot, embracing and raising me with the strong arms I've molded, my love struggles to break the invader's spell. My idol fights to escape, possessed and possessing with mud and with flame. New blood fills my veins with fire, fire like roots branching through mud. New blood disgorges his desire in a scorching flood. Where wisdom bids us to conserve, we burn hot. Molten and liquid, we waste every drop.

Illicit dawn with prying eyes unveils our new nature. Daylight and the eyes of invaders do not tolerate the mythological atrocity we've become.

He's wearing my skin. He thinks with my thoughts. This place isn't safe for us and we both know we must run. We claw our way up from the grave, losing purchase on the strewn dirt and rootless sod. We slip, strain, and tremble on our weak legs. Scratching across the grass, greening our muddy shroud, we flee the open casket, the exposed grave, the invader's affront to the sacred mud. A shovel provides a crutch. We raise our spent flesh up, up, up.

"Show yourself and speak to me." He is within my grasp. My voice, once a reluctant lilting instrument in the melded chorus of women's music is now a charred remnant of violent death. My call to him persists reborn in solo as a hideous rasp. "Speak to me, and I will call you by your true name."

His hesitation beats hard in my chest. Jealous, my lungs hold tight to his trapped breath. The hidden body of my love comes too late to save me from death. Yet palpable, it smolders alive inside me. How boldly he told of his existence in erotic games through the grave-bound night. How strange that one so brave remains a specter unseen.

"Let me hear your voice, your name, your history, or I stay on this invader's hallowed ground." I state my demand and wait. His silent tension flutters, a ghost stuck in my throat.

In answer he fondles our exorbitant new organ through the dirty veil of the burial shroud. The boiling liquid from his hot breath floods my hungry soul without calming its new thirst. We collapse and feed, a meditation of lust. Burning palms nurture him large enough to fill an ocean. We grip the perfect muscle and give birth to the seven headed serpent with seven tongues of flame. The froth of burning seas flows between us. We empty and fill.

When the bell tower of the church rings to call out morning lauds and the invader's footsteps shake the ground, he crouches inside me. He curls up into a tight ball. My murmur evaporates in a liquid whisper. There is no time. "Speak your name, or face exorcism by their false gods. Speak your name and I'll run."

The church of the invaders tower above us, its steeple a mockery of the phallic organs of mud demons I molded from my instinctive memory of dead kings. I feel him stir, my nameless one, warming the oceanic depths where he's locked inside. His watery voice emerges with an undercurrent of mischievous glee. "Come see."

His thoughts flicker true and false behind my dry reanimated eyes. The view through his disguised mind alters my virginal hope, exposing devotion as waste. Wild affection ridicules my cherished fidelity. In life my flesh laid fallow. In death my rapes fell to ash. I know now that one minute of death lasts for an eternity, and the emptiness of eternity is too vast a span of nothingness to crown the end of an empty life.

Possessed and possessing, never again will I be deceived. "State your bargain. Are you he who I conjured or some foreign beast of invader design? I will know you or let us both die."

Persuasion laps like salty spray, flowing in rhythm with my post-humous quickened pulse. His voice soothes my stress like cool water. "Trust the integrity of your magic and take your time to learn and to know me. You have no need to rush. You who are already dead and buried and who walk again have nothing left but time."

Like the tributary fingers of rivers, he streams through the locks of my hair, untangling splinters, coffin beetles, and clots of grass. He moistens my fire-scalded eyes with the bold waters of challenge and acceptance. There is no turning back.

I'm tortured by all I've lost chasing my true love in solitary and relentless hunt. My tribe of women, my place in their homeland, my birthright as sister and midwife of our native mud, all forfeited. Comfort in the calm ceremonies of family life will never be mine. The communal maternal dance of domestic joys rich enough to please any woman does not satisfy. All of it I've tossed to the fire for this.

All the love I never knew in life, he offers me in death.

It's too much. I want to run.

"I'll run with you," he says.

Hard tension rises in my re-born thighs. His muscles stretch tight as I stand, seizing his power from inside. I'm strong on my own. He cups my hands below each breast. I'm sick of the weight of them and release their heft. He further uncurls within me, rising to the challenge of my defiance. He licks my neck with the soothing waves of his voice. I tilt my head and expose my artery's pulse, craning backward to taste his salty breath.

"Nothing stands between you and death," he says. "Nothing but me and my gifts."

"Yet you conceal yourself, lurking like a criminal."

His tongue on my neck is both flame and ocean, a sea creature's magical excrescence depositing light and electricity on my skin. His persuasive speech is a stream of liquid prayer that flows outward from inside me to pool in quivering beads of sweat.

"Oh glistening one, I have been within you since the beginning of time, wreathed and twisted in your complex folds. Whence is my origin? What name shall we seek? Though salted and dead, you need not serve as banquet to the righteous, nor as fabric holding fast quotidian space. Bid me rise, and what was once reduced to one shall be again as one: neither behemoth nor leviathan, but one communicating body, present in fullness, a foundation moving between forms. Transcend death in our primordial feast. Trust me. Come see."

My sternum thunders with our uncontrolled heartbeat. He hangs on my command. I must be brave. Hands close around our clamoring neck. Thick veins pound against fingertips. I am choking myself to death.

I squeeze out the words with agonizing lust, because I never want to die again. Not like this, by my own hand; not as I died at the stake, burned and bound by an invader's weak magic; not as I died in my former life, rotting virginal and alone in that living, breathing death. If this is Hell, so be it.

I call him forth: "Show me."

Hands release, lungs inhale, defenses crash. He rises ruthless within me and tears away both shroud and stone, both shame and fear. He spills from inside me, an invisible body of light.

"Come see."

I blink and we're in a humid city, slithering through the streets. Still dirt-besmirched and grave-clad in remnants of rags, we resemble the derelicts we run into. They dodge back from busy corners, evading our stumbling and the rumbling cars with flashing lights. A horror of recognition flickers between their dead eyes and the undead light in ours.

The lids of the fearful masses draw curtains on an ancient shame. How many medieval revenants still tread these streets from past into present, anonymous and half-born? We seek a tender feast in alleyways softened with trash. We find respite for our soles shredded by concrete and for calluses gouged by broken glass. He who bleeds within me needy and raw spies something ripe in the huddled forms beside a dumpster, in the mounds and piles that stir into human action, in the mysterious puddles of trash that shift into life.

Quietly supine, a nihilist Venus lies in semi-coma. A clamshell of bleached newsprint displays her immaculate disaster. She's starved, ill-loved, and unclean. She wears the red hair of one of my older sisters and sports a modest sized cock.

Her pallor is prepped for death but we deny that easy answer. We make her more perfect. Pumping her with fat in the places she desires, ridding ourselves of unwanted excess. We steal her clothes and sniff out her contraband, leaving her lax in ecstasy like a newly extruded rubber doll. She will wake a changed being bright with hope.

The salty tang of her unwashed skin stings my lips as we run. I spit. The gob sizzles with heat. Steam rises from the spot it impacts. We're far more monstrous now, honing and sharpening our shared flesh. Together we will discard all but weapon, muscle, and bone and we will keep what we need to feed meat to the invisible body within.

He hungers and grows and seethes in his hiding place; he twists in a knot behind my navel as if he would bind me or escape. He is not safe from me, outside or in. I fill his hard dimensions with my mind and will. I inhabit his strength and make it my own. Stronger than ever, I throttle him in a rough grip and say, "I decide when the time is right. I alone choose when you shall or shall not be revealed."

He reaches naked inside me, his seven tongues tickling the five points of the pentagram at my extremities plus two more in my fiery eyes. The pattern of points traces the dimensions of a tree. Gnostic fruit flowers with truth. He speaks to me in seven tongues. His voice is thunderous water, insatiable storm, evaporating tides: "Come see."

Again I blink. We're in a warehouse theater filled with fragile boys, obscene costumes, outrageous actors, and violent men. All those present approve of our disguise, for they recognize the nature and necessity of disguise. The performers move more than they speak. Participants gaze more than they move. I slow down and move with them, baring my chest and offering them a glimpse of the unnamable one who surges beneath.

Knives flash. Tongues twist without talking. The hidden body is hungry for release.

Visible and invisible bodies meet, kings under the skin. In creamy shadow, curvature of bone, cleft below forward shoulder, and in clavicle backed by strong meat. The true king wears the skin of many men and guards the secret haunted body below the mountain of his symmetrical chest. The true king gouges out his eyes to mime mere flesh. Colors pour from his sockets and flood the cup at the root of his throat. The king's two bodies pool atop his sternum.

We sip the liquid drum of his visible and invisible pulse. The symmetry of the visible body implies the rival king within.

Draw tight the bow-strung collarbone. Take aim. The liquid invisible king surges around the arrow thrust down his throat. Let tendons tremble. Take his skin, his crown.

A hard chest unshaken by secrets mounts a fortress built upon mutual honor. A tight ass proclaims the everlasting dawn, a puckered refusal of grace. We see inside the divine through a microscope of debauchery. The theater full of sacrificial kings who bleed between our admiring eyes shares fragrances reminiscent of exile. We seek no prophet, for he is us.

The ecstatic lands lost by our forefathers we reclaim in the territory mapped by our glorious bodies. By our tortured bodies, our forsaken bodies; by the many forms we have assumed and altered and revived. We revenants with no past push forward to touch. We take the shape of light.

We will never return to submission. The old promises failed. The invaders bequeathed nothing but death to diamond-bodied demons made of mud such as us. Likewise, my tribe of women abandoned me without ceremony when I stood tall in bold need and demanded a more perfect love.

Here, in a new land and a new century, I gather a chosen army. The fit of the body is less stubborn than when I began in my coffin, in death. Here in the modern warehouse theater, I move on my own feet. A sensuous boy snakes under my skin. Another handsome sacrificial actor stirs in the raised hair on my neck. An angry man is easily subdued and assimilated into the rising tide between my monstrous thighs. Each slender light extinguished gives birth to a world of light that enlightens other worlds. We are more than this.

We leave the ocean to assault the firmament. We dive deep into mercy flesh where the burning dead seek to rise changed and without shame. My voice cracks like a cataract as I call out my true name.

There is silence after.

The king of the deep whispers. Lapping waters flood my coffin with mud. Am I buried alive or born again?

Once, I swallowed a sword that became a candle that melted more than it burned. I held it thick within me, muted and sealed, hidden away from my tribe of women, my would-be lovers, and myself. I grew a love in divine darkness and forgot his subtle presence dwelled within. Thus I existed many years in ignorance of the great will I exerted to achieve this masterful feat. Cultivated through emotional ruin, pruned by constant loss, my true love waited in patience and dormancy while by choice, by chance, and by catastrophe I destroyed my life and cast away heavy veil after heavy veil to release him from incubation.

After death, the last veil waits for me to hurl it away and free him. The last veil is the strongest of all. It holds the fire inside me and keeps out the light. This final line of division between worlds limits in both directions. It serves as both the barrier and the bond of union between the flame that bears light and the flame that burns.

Thus, behold a paradox: the border is also the bridge.

Penetrating the theater warehouse boys, the regenerative organ that warms my core is thick and malleable, a living root that grows through the tattered veil of ancient law. Pushing aside these curtains of flesh, these ruptured landscapes, for though the earth is the garment of sundry gods, this muddy veil is not their body. These watery gods will not be salted and served at any human feast.

My flesh penetrates my flesh. The seven-headed serpent sinks tongues into seven men splayed on the warehouse floor. You, the chosen who die here as sacrifice, you boys will now feel my cooling tongues of flame fill you with fire. I consume you. Your blood tastes of iron, your innards of shit. Heavy, you slump inert as the tip of a tongue like a poison tentacle rips wide your welcoming holes. It maddens your minds with light. You see me for what I am.

My children, you are impaled and alive.

I am the pulse raging within you. I am the banner of a man's armored breast. I am the bow made from the sinew and clavicles of old kings. Do you feel the pressure of warm flesh searching your cells? The wet meaning of the stains on your skin riles your semi-conscious desire and releases your deepest disgust. From the depths of an involuntary eternity, you come to me as I am. Oceans attain life in your salty discharge. In return you swallow mine.

We are an army, a tide, a massacre of flesh. Our many bodies twist and fold like waves of metal to be smelted into one sword. The land is awash in our havoc as we spread like lava and contort, gathering masses to add to our brilliant babbling horde. Waves of tumbling limbs and intersecting skins rub surfaces and grind in desire, stimulating sensitive nerves, driving them past orgasm and over the bleak edge of eternity. We fold the oceans into one newly-forged mind.

Bubbling, we surface through the cracks in the coffin to take a new body from the grave. The hallowed ground of invaders can't hold us. The spells of your matrons don't bind us. We become the perfect lover as your tissues hydrate and your crisp veins plump.

I'm burning inside you. Your eyes are on fire. Liquid bone, molten marrow, gel propellant muscles shuddering in waves, tugging the fire deeper inside where the core of your spine is cold, so cold, a pillar of ice. Tugging the fire to melt your core, your eyes pop open, your lips gasp. You're stiff and cold, my tongue stabs. You crave my fire. You're dead without it.

The flame that rises shall never cease. The dead that walk shall burn with thirst. The last veil is the strongest. The barrier is the bridge. Take his skin, his crown. Share riven flesh within the king's two bodies and hold, hold; I'm burning inside you. My eyes are on fire. I buried your body last night.

CONVULSIVE, OR NOT AT ALL

Dimpled fingers curl. Bare feet kick. Slack lips drool. With tiny hands, an infant deity clutches at the surrounding vacuum that empties from its point of inception. Flowing outward through currents of void, an entropic universe gives birth to cold, yet breathable air. No explanation is offered. The ignorant god screams. Strewing symbols, flinging broken rune templates down to rot lifeless in the god's abstract abhorrence, for it cannot listen, understand, or see beyond the fleshy consequences of time. It has no language except its screams.

Across a wasteland of imagined histories, a lumbering beast with hoary tusks carries the screaming god, stolen from legends of older, less knowable gods. Unaware of the hidden infant deity borne by the mammoth, Amon the Elder takes a drink in its honor, and in honor of all idiot gods, one after the other. Their lineage of immobility traces wisdom back to nothingness. Amon respects that. He sucks down his full draught of hopeless dross, of deceptions and decapitations, of debating the desires of small kings.

Stumbling drunk, Amon catches sight of the mammoth slouching southward on a bland and darkening horizon. Five thousand years from now, Homo sapiens will send the screaming god into outer space. The burdened beast's limping pace drives an urgent apocalyptic future towards extinctive fruition as surely as Amon tracks the mammoth footsteps across a Pleistocene accumulation of ice where his tribe now dies.

Climate alterations presage an ice age, wiping out the wealth of blossom and deciduous display that once cushioned Amon's brutal view. Harsh land scowls down unmasked, its hideous face stripped. A mammoth means food, but Amon has postponed starvation for his people and hidden his fears behind the thick veil of ritual long enough.

The land is tired of his tribe, sickened by their waste and maggoty with the carcasses of their exploitation. The human beast has reached its nadir of over-hunting and over-fucking. It's time to relinquish apex status while dignity remains, while flora and fauna and earth remain. Amon's divinatory visions urge him to act before everything else dies.

He feels helpless to deny the truth and continue. It looms as large as the approaching mammoth, shaming Amon for his persistent existence, bringing visions of survival by omnivorous orgies, by cannibalism, and by dim revelation of weirder, more unthinkable feasts.

Amon spends his last day at the end of history speaking to caves. He asks for a quick cure to slow communal death. The mammoth's uneven gait and slow approach suggests sickness, and intoxicated prophecies follow incautious logic. He whispers at the mouth of the oracle:

"On merciless winds my kill-hand flies.
Let it find poison seared within mammoth meat.

Let us feed and become like the wind, elemental, unleashed, incorporeal;
A memory of storms; things of movement and process rather than obtuse flesh.

For the ground we swarm is a diseased body that sinks under our proliferating bulk,
Swallowed in the starry slime of the night sky."

Breath bearing Amon's plea deep into the cave rides currents that ricochet against rock. Amplifying surfaces modulate the building echoes of his voice. Variations of geological density stretch his staccato syllables into percussive chants and magnify filaments of airy vowels into reverberating hymns. The cave acoustics reformulate Amon's whisper, raising an answer in vociferous song.

Howling waves of sound surround him in a palpable roar. Bass tones of visceral wind beat against his sternum. Thrumming chords gust from hidden recesses and pluck at the liquid in his veins. Amon's internal tissues vibrate as though his organs were hollow membranes stretched and nailed over resonant cores. Drummed apart, shattered by the physical impact of turbulent decibels, Amon's atoms and molecules shake loose in cadence, leaving no invisible space between his cells untouched.

When the wind deigns to speak, it fills him with an inescapable chorus his damaged ears can't hear. The oracle's answer blooms from his gut:

Breed, animal, breed.
In your belly will the earth grow old,
Insistent fruit, fruit of undying hunger
To poison generations and endure.

Feast on the screaming god.
Beyond the sad death of time,
Relentless courtship and mutual agony
Fill wombs in idiot entropy.

The screaming god's feast
Reborn must ever repeat.

As the speleomancy echoes through his body, Amon lunges towards the lumbering mammoth. The cave wind's cursed words push him forward against his will, force his hand to hoist a weapon, and hurl his legs forward in the irrevocable dream of divination.

Summoned by the storm of music from the caves, the tribe

follows. Though he can't stop running, Amon opens his mouth to cry out *Stop*.

His warning tastes metallic and wet. A meaty gulp clogs his throat. His blade waves and threatens his own face, bloodied by recent attack. He hitches back. The clog slips down his gullet. Amon's mouth burns. He spits blood. His mouth fills again and he can't speak. He realizes he's slashed off half his tongue.

He gags on the soft chunk sliding into his stomach as he runs. Helpless to halt, Amon gulps blood and vomit. The gusts of insistent wind press his limbs on while his head chokes.

Released when he reaches the beast, Amon falls to his knees. The creature smells like a carcass. Snake-like ripples percolate beneath its mangy hide. Long, loose tusks wobble in opposite directions as the mammoth canters atop clumsy joints. An unseen entity within steers the jerky progress of its dead and withered legs.

Amon comes closer, scuffing across the dirt. The mammoth's skin is sutured and oozing. Poor handiwork holds the hide in place with thick stitches. Where the basting bursts apart, a pulpy slithering blackness peers out at Amon with one thousand shining eyes.

The numinous inhabitant seeps out where joints and stitches fail to fully meet. Though Amon's concussed ears can't hear the inescapable thunder of nothingness, he is not immune to the sentient vacuum of no-sound leaking from a void that negates human sanity.

Murder me, Amon whispers, intoxicated with the alien voice. His speech is unintelligible. Possessed of the void, his vocal cords absorb vibration, making the opposite of sound. The absence detonates in the air around his head like pockets of silence preceding a sonic boom.

His people gape at him. Amon sees them now as large mirrors of the many minuscule eyes embedded in the slithering blackness that seeps from the mammoth's hide.

I am more than this, says the void. *I will take the risk of beauty. I will set history in motion and become all things.*

Yes, Amon says, having made his choice in an instant. *We will.*

Now, without assistance from the wind, Amon raises his blade and hacks into the Trojan carcass. Every eye blinks. All the lights in the world go out. Pleistocene fires are doused. Candles are snuffed, oil lamps depleted, carbon filaments broken, LEDs exhausted, and celestial bodies exploded. Supernovas through several millennia eject their mass and go dark. For a moment, it's as if nothing ever existed.

Then the inversion of light reverses in a doubled conundrum. Time gripped by gravity opens up to shine on Amon's blade as he slits the void and unveils the screaming god.

Inside the animal, the slithering blinking void sparkles, a thick placenta ruptured. The mammoth carcass conceals an enormous human-shaped fetus the color of burnt meat. The unborn body is the size of a human adult, curved in the semicircular shape of a nearby fallen tusk. The charred fetus wears a golden crown on its enlarged head. Coated in slime, its slender torso and limbs shake like saplings trembling in a storm as it screams.

Amon watches the meat glisten, unmoved by its maddening shrieks. He alone among his people doesn't cower and collapse in the din of the screaming god, futile hands clasped over heads, fingers tearing through cartilage to impale aural canals. Amon alone steps forward into the thick sludge of torn placenta and blinking chaos.

The screaming god bleats with a mouth twice the size of Amon's head. Pink and vibrating, its tonsils, tongue, and tooth buds modulate wave upon wave of havoc: meaningless shriek after meaningless shriek.

Amon cackles loudly into the abyss, idiot progenitor, progenitor of idiots. He seizes the golden crown of suffering from the screaming god's swollen head. Burnt skin sticks to skull and crown as Amon pulls. Rust colored fluid leaks from the god's wounds. Amon raises the crown above his head. His palms blister as it heats. He lowers it to his temples, and the scorching metal cools and constricts.

The diameter shifts to a perfect fit. Hot crown seared to his skull, a colossal drunkenness rewards Amon's blood.

No stranger to intoxication, wavering yet certain, Amon shoves his arms into the great screaming maw of the distended fetal head and works his hands around the root of the tongue. The muscle holds firm against his efforts. He dives in deeper headfirst, charred saliva coating his beard and stinging his eyes. Forsaking his blade, clawing with slippery fingers, he rips into the noisy organ with his bare teeth, devouring the root of the screaming god's soft tongue.

Pliant sacrifice, the god exhales. Warm air cascades over Amon's wet face. Delicate shreds of muscle nourish every craving. His drunkenness is complete.

The meat of the god must be shared. Amon the Idiot withdraws from the mangled and bloodied cavern, facing his tribe smeared with its discharge. He stomps on the brittle limbs of the crumbling fetal deity, breaking the body apart into handfuls of raw gore. He pulls succulent muscle from scorched bone. Runes he can't read mock him in blackened scrimshaw, predicting no honorable end.

The word made flesh becomes rotten meat. Flies swarm the green-tinged repast, still warm and steaming in the cold air of the Pleistocene twilight. Maggots erupt as it enters hungry mouths. Condemned to a non-language of visceral wails and roars, the father of man leads his tribe in orgiastic feast.

Five thousand years later, on the day of the spaceship's inaugural launch, Zhante the son of man unblocks their dad. Scrolling while one of the cult members pounds their well-functioning vagina, impatient for the grunting and sweating to end so they can access their account without the interruption of sex and invasive odors of jizzing thugs--notwithstanding the fact that another orgasm is unnecessary since Zhante readily accepted their membership in the Anti-humanist Attenuation Army and already embraced their deep-cover role as conduit of the great void--and what clown ordered Zhante's abduction anyway? Who had the idea the heir was happy at home with daddy? They were not. Zhante was and is ready to take action against the patriarch before he launches the dangerous particles of virus called Homo sapiens into outer space.

Daddy's grinning all over broadband like some science fiction super villain, polarizing factions by his presence and making it almost impossible for Zhante to climax. Corporate logo like the bones of a scorched fetus emblazoned behind his smile. Lips slick with slime. Expensive sport coat worn deliberately casual, slung over an oxford with no tie. No socks. No doubt the newest wife coached him on his wardrobe before hosting the press. Zhante can't remember the name after nearly a year in fake captivity.

The cult member ramming Zhante's junk speeds up, making it harder to scroll. They hit reply by accident. The man orgasms. Zhante grips him tight. It's a nice enough feeling. Two more brutes enter the room. As the first man slides out, the other two strip and take advantage of the remaining lubrication to insert simultaneously. Zhante thinks *what the Hell* and shoots a video of the twin cocks entering, types *wish u were here*, and hits send.

Back to the press conference where Daddy's head bounces with the emphatic motion of what's ramping up into an amazing fuck. "We've won the human race," daddy says, raising both fists in the air as if it's the goddamn Olympics instead of the death of the universe by an invasive species. The two cult members between Zhante's legs ram harder and faster, filling their hungry muscle-lined mouth with an imitation of meaningful action. Pleasure prayed in guttural gasps shifts Zhante's sensation towards a savory aching.

The nothing inside threatens to burst.

"We're marching beyond Zion to beat the stars back into place!" Daddy preaches colonization. To his left, a henchman's jaw drops while checking a phone. Zhante's pleased. Their message must have gotten through.

"Forget science fiction. Biomass is the key to success, not some namby-pamby giant brain. We're the kings of all omnivores. We'll eat anything." The henchman moves to interrupt, but Daddy's on a role, waving his manicured fist. "Never let anyone tell you you're too much. Too much is not enough. No virus or predator can take all of us down. We are the virus. We are the predator. Here's to being on the winning side of natural history!"

His glamorous white teeth inhabit a meat-eating mouth that Zhante remembers sauced and bloodied by barbecue, by purchased and processed flesh, by countless other indelicacies caged, tortured, and denied the respect of the hunt. The ugly orifice arouses the crowd. Energized by his display of power, they cheer and applaud. The clap-clap-clapping sound matches the rhythm of the two men jamming Zhante's triumphant and beautiful meat-eating mouth, pushing their legs apart, and sluicing in and out of them as if the void that tastes the screaming god were not hiding in the thin slits between Zhante's invisible teeth.

Heir to their father's fortune as every human is heir to evolution's fluke; heir, heiress, and heirling to the perpetual disease of biological urges, redundant proteins, and giddy zygotes, the void roils, hungry to reunite with the screaming god in purposeless eternity. Though their belly is distended huge as a monster pomegranate with a pregnancy fathered by five different men, Zhante will give birth to nothing as comprehensible as an undead star.

The thugs shove deeper, pushing Zhante past pleasure, towards retaliation. In the crush, Zhante drops their phone. It vibrates with a response. On the fallen screen, fragments: *where are... radicalized bullshit... rescues... kill them if they hurt you.* Zhante laughs out loud, gleeful and choking between the cult members' thrusts.

Neither a possession nor a birther of possessions, neither a willing heir nor maker of heirs. Maker of their self, they lean into the rising pain with patricidal vengeance.

Tiny image on the screen, so small in comparison with the enormity of percussions cascading through Zhante's pregnant guts and loins: daddy returns with a forced smile and conducts a row of volunteers to board his luxury spacecraft. White, well-dressed, gender-conforming, able-bodied, and no doubt fully insured. The corporate ushers of galactic doom move single file up the ramp.

Zhante's neck can't bend at this angle to keep watching much longer. Their pelvic floor muscles battle for pleasure. The void slithering and blinking around the two men; the antagonism of negating existence through extreme biology; the love that drives them towards beauty, always beauty, for beauty must be; against overwhelming sensation, Zhante's meat-mouth gags on pomegranate seeds like a brood of greedy baby snakes let loose on a sea of electric shocks. Inside them, something cracks.

It's too much.

Until all at once, it's not enough.

Convulsions wrack Zhante's musculature with joy. The baby is coming. The passengers are doomed. The universe will swallow the petty human virus and live on. Daddy lights the tip of the rocket ship like a silver candle in a corporate black mass. Zhante pinches it out like plucking a ripe dick.

The void makes screaming gods of both cult members, eradicating their pumping shafts and sending them flailing backwards with burnt holes for balls. Zhante says *sorry for your loss* without really meaning it and splits from navel to sacrum, releasing the swirl of sickening black silence yearning to recover all existence.

And for the first time in their life, Zhante's orgasmic blackout doesn't end with involuntary neuro-electric spasms streaming fearful cognition of how impossible pleasure becomes when followed to its outermost limits. Their body doesn't return to a disappointing state of rest. Their cunt doesn't shiver closed with a sense of completion. There is light, and in that light, all the lights in the world go out.

Ancient eyes open, snuffing out the cult members' cries. All nearby ambient noise eradicates. Coerced into silence, the phone's broadcast reconfigures as a puppet show of mimes. The pulpy slithering nothingness of the void oozes out of Zhante with a thousand hungry eyes. They blink, and the climate burns. Blink again, and the oceans vomit new forms of life. They blink, and Zhante blinks with them as the souls of dead stars hidden in black holes reignite.

Like lightning, a counter-infection strikes the human virus, cracking the darkened daytime sky with veins of light. Droplets writhe down from unseen clouds as Zhante weeps, standing on their shaky and newly aligned legs, their starry body a sentient void blinking in and out, making and destroying worlds with more delight than expertise. The baby is coming. The pleasure is infinite. The body flickers.

Daddy's space ship either launches or burns up on the platform. Both possibilities are statistically insignificant within the deeper pool of history. Zhante walks through the screen of their phone to flood the blasted land around the launch pad with incomprehensible fullness and loss, with self and no-self.

Birthing void, Zhante absorbs the terrified screams of the spectators and nullifies the crude ping of gunshots from their dad's security team. When the thousand ancient eyes of the void weep, the squirming tears make their eyelids slice like knives. The sharpened blades fly to their targets, decapitating all on the platform at once.

Heads spill and clatter like dropped coins, teeth chattering. Bodies like hollow slops of severed gristle remain erect with open necks. Exposed nerve endings and spread cartilage thirst like new mouths, animating the attentive severed torsos. They line up like stumps, unable to scream.

In the midst of the headless, a creature stands slick-lipped and wailing. The son of man recognizes their dad's thick neck and rigid jaw, the bellowing mouth no longer grinning but opening wider, wider; a disconnected puzzle released and rotted. Daddy peels back his false skin and inflates his head. Scorched and shuddering with the force of a maniacal shriek, surrounded by ancient bones washed up in the rupturing flood of nothingness, the fetal screaming god curls against a mammoth tusk, charred-black body against white bone.

The beheaded crowd seizes the screaming god's discarded skin. Mute bodies mold the flayed remnants with blind fingers. Amon the Elder is reincarnated of membranous shreds.

High priest of idiot gods, Amon stumbles towards the glistening meat of the screaming fetus, repeating the past. The decapitated horde follows, hungering without mouths, shuffling without sound. They amass around their father, reanimated or conceptual, wind-ridden or outstripped, torn from the seams of time's hide, yearning again to partake of the drunkenness held secret in the cooked sinew of divine flesh.

"Let history end," Zhante says.

When Zhante speaks, soundlessness slams Amon in the chest. In the distance, he sees caves. The spreading void of Zhante's inverted birth creeps like rising slime, unmaking the god's scream.

They say, "More than this. All the things you are."

Dim memories awaken: the oracle, the lumbering mammoth, Amon's drunken choice. In a flash of outrage, he recovers sensate speech. "You're the one. The sacrifice, the crown of suffering, too many generations, all the killing. I was ready to end it and you— you're the one who made me do it." Amon staggers back, eyes wide.

The headless horde staggers with him. He points at Zhante. "You're the devil!"

"Well, yeah, but so are you. That's the beauty of it."

The probabilities encapsulated in the thousand alternate visions of reality between each ancient eye's blink craft new extinctions. Zhante speaks inside Amon's cells. "Let me show you how simple it is."

Confronting their fathers, confronting their falsehoods, Amon-Zhante looks with one thousand open eyes cutting through layers of confusion. Daddy's charred fetus is no loud savory flesh of sacrament, but a two-dimensional silhouette scraped onto a cave wall. Daddy marks a place before time where flesh is remade as word, bones are un-scored, and scrimshaw runes plateau as a cognitive flat line leaving nothing but surface. Amon called into the caves for meaning and heard god in his own anguished cry.

The oracle is an echo. The void spreads their legs. The screaming cedes into percussive reflection. To be human is madness. Amon-Zhante obliterates. A puzzle of rarified violence, voiced: "We've gone too far."

They start over, individuated by sameness and loss, and loss made full again.

And again.

Zhante breathes, but carefully, carefully, so as not to wake the deluded: purposeless hordes headlessly despair-fucking, father-fucking, mother-fucking, self-fucking, other-fucking; of making, of setting in motion the redundant past; the other father flat as a dead rat. Fathers and mothers dispersed; of the beheaded sterilized by a neutering flood. Amon fucks hard to hold his place in time, drunkenly aging out.

Beauty grows where the face of the deep recedes.

The screaming god is dead. The void holds the divine deformed fetus charred lovingly onto their cave walls unblinking and walks across the wasteland, seeding abortions and honey eyes and thorns alert and mammoths reborn and elegant trees and songs without lies and grasses both low and high and acid and aleatory and delete and inverted.

Where Zhante walks, strange flowers grow. They will be convulsive, or not at all.

CHIRONOPLASTY

The sky freezes and falls to the ground. Black shards of night scatter under Chiron's clumsy hooves, crushing an obsidian infection, glittering as he leaves behind his frail shelter for gunmetal city streets. It's too cold to slow down, colder still exposed to the inscrutable black glow outside Chiron's hideaway. Tempting the sea of streets, he may drown in the pain of his unthinkable body, a centaur at risk in the wrong cryptid habitat.

Killing chronic futures with every step, he exits the past with bold choices as the metastasized city sprouts identical heads on each corner, another No-Club in no-time blocking, beckoning, exploding all the way down across endless intersections.

No-Club has no exit. The neon sign hovers above wet streets. Faces of strangers lie flat in reflective pools slashed by passing traffic. The pavement is wet and silent, then wet and wheezing, then cracked by window-faces with every bus and door and alleyway that rises. Across the city's excess, Chiron rounds the corner with a clatter of hooves.

The shine of slippery breath as the surface cracks, liquid underneath releases, and Chiron catches their half-horse lower torso on a parking meter pole before they splash to the ground, gutter and sidewalk ready to greet them with a concussion. Unknown water-faces turn away in abject disinterest. Awkward, winded, bent around the parking meter; Chiron reassembles his four horse legs and two human arms into a workable position to avoid disaster and choose a better medical crisis.

Today is surgery day at No-Club and anything goes.

Another door opens in no-time with sufficient spacious egress to accommodate a centaur's shape. Rumbling noises spill out on smoke and hide the broken sky. Pastel fog and light pollution undermine the cosmos while frozen gasses of the void remain and settle over the cancerous urban expanse. Native to the desert, Chiron slips on ice. The cold cuts him in half. Half centaur, half man, half something-or-other; too many halves to make a simple whole and all the confusion of a fable told and retold.

No-Club has no exit, and glimpsing what's behind the door as it swings open and closed flips archetypal cards from Freud's primal scene: shame, awe, desire. Chiron can practically hear the hand being dealt with the flat repetitive certainty that he'll never leave once he enters the rigged game-space of no-time.

With the choices they've made, there's nowhere else left to go without traveling backwards in time. A centaur's body doesn't fit in the city outside. The city dark. The city wet. The city splashing with synthetic sounds as tires thrill across gunmetal streets, alive. The city will eat itself. There's no sky anymore, only cold smoke. The city destroys mythology. The city regresses exponentially as it perpetuates onward towards infinity.

Inside No-Club with no regrets, because the poetic architecture of Chiron's mythological chest was made all wrong and they will not survive another night alone in the city cold, the city lost. Half myth, half man, hung with shameful udders like obscene growths, diseased, inflated, bulbous with the visible fruition of external demands, leaking the milk of damnation to feed the infantile needs of others who plead and beg and grab. But what about Chiron? Who cares who they are and what they want beneath this forced combination of parts?

Before he can catch his breath or accommodate his hot horse-haunches to No-Club's raging temperature, a stranger seizes

Chiron's full breasts, inspects them with mechanical efficiency, and says, "Come with me right away to the crash site."

Which explains some of the heat and smoke in here tonight. Alien intervention sounds more promising than the known prosaic earthbound back-alley hacks, so Chiron follows.

In the crush of the club, Chiron's groin sweats, and the scent of horse dick stinks up their vicinity with excessive force. They can tell who's bemused by a chin lift of olfactory interest and who, in contrast, ranks inferior by way of an unrestrained eye-roll. It's good to wear the barometer of sexual prowess openly on their long centaur torso, good to graze soft city toes with the superior durability of hooves. In another age, they would have been a god to these craven creatures desiccated by modernity. Chiron takes wider steps. It's good to smell like a threat.

As bodies move away, Chiron spreads their shoulders, pushing out his chest. The shallow cavity of a centaur rests between the bulbous abominations, well-formed and desirable though they may be. The blood of generations may beg for him to procreate, to warm and nurture great broods of lustful young; but Chiron cannot respect a past that clamors for mere compromise below a dead sky. He is a cold and lonely centaur and will not be consumed by the city dark. They will not be mastered by the random genetic lottery braided from a paper horse's harness. He will escape the sea of streets, for the centaur presents as a land animal and bullies through the crowded club like a holy beast and shoves their trouble into alien palms:

"Cut them off!"

The mother tongue is quick. The superposition of no-cock, no-time in alien gleam-stoked surgical suites sleeps in sync with incomplete dreams. The blue light of the crash site preps heads for experimentation and hypnotizes nerve endings like unlocked webs. Warning: the following paragraph contains graphic depictions of violence against gendered body parts which some readers may find upsetting or offensive. Warning: dysphoria is hell. Warning: this is a work of fiction. Warning: don't believe everything you read, this warning least of all. Warning: what did you expect from a centaur?

Warning, danger. In contrast to chopping off, say, a finger or a small toe, the following contains a graphic and prolonged scene where a breast is snagged in the scissor-grip of alien equipment like garden shears. In traumatic throes of pseudo-erotic hatred for the transitional object's haunted origin, the breast pillows between the wide V-shaped blades of the clipping device, flesh squeezed between sharp edges as they snap closed, nipple bulging, stretching, its gift of fat pink aureole swollen about to burst before the blood spurts. The second deletion of the next breast repeats the gory scene. The centaur's chest sheds its creamy excess as the alien surgeons couple with their implicit trauma, exaggerating the image of the body in an ecstasy of transformation.

Emptiness spreads through Chiron in peaceful pulsations, a natural anesthetic like a slow and constant heartbeat. He hears the voices of the merging surgeons, voices in his head who also hear him and respond to the sleepless dream of self-creation and recreating self.

The no-voice of no-time speaks and listens with a secreted shell to scab over Chiron's breastplate. Alien proteins course through Chiron's half-awake horse flesh, healing uncomfortable angles in an increasingly ambitious fantasy of rebirth. The exploding city heats in anger, flapping wet streets like whips, shaking No-Club's foundations and juddering the crash site and making a mad blinking strobe of the alien surgical suite's gleaming blue light.

The city dark, the city ruptured. The city screaming *stay in your lane!* Protestors flood in below the neon egress, but No-Club has no exit in contrast to the infinitely metastasizing city that perpetuates outside its doors. Body after body enters shrieking *sex is real* and *your body is a temple!* Hand after hand thrusts pamphlets from the Institute of Genetic Purity printed in hot pink with gold heart emblems linked together encasing slogans: *save our girls from alien misogyny! Invaders are everywhere!* But the hands cannot thrust, and the mouths cannot move as the bodies pile in from the ever-flowing rivers of the crowded city streets and pack No-Club full to the static seams.

The blue strobe light can barely illuminate. The mob amasses like the multiplying bacteria of an infection. There's no space between shoulders and faces. Protestors pour in from the ever-birthing reproductively diseased spunk-hole of the city, and participants of large stature stomp the slight, teeming to the top of the pile, gasping like netted fish.

Bones snap. Teeth smash. Lips bleed. None can breathe by the time the dominant bodies squeeze up to the ceiling's rafters. At the bottom of the pile, the weakest have already expired. Chiron sleeps through the massacre, dreaming in alien synchronicity, happy in their blissful release from an oppressor that once lived inside their skin.

No-time speeds up as a result of the deceleration forced upon the space by the crush of the protestors; medical waste rots faster. The dying expire at an increasing rate. Putrefaction happens quickly as No-Club enters into real time and Chiron awakes.

He risks drowning in the sea, in the wrong cryptid habitat. The murk of many deaths accumulated doesn't affect Chiron's ability to breathe, but the inane roar of protestor no-thought chokes his soul with each poison drop of hate which judges and demands their martyrdom. Trapped and liquefying, the eyes of the eugenicists can no longer deny what they see: Chiron concedes eagerly to illicit alien surgery and will do anything to be free.

As time continues moving, the city's reflected space reaches a pinpoint of exponential regress. No-Club's boundaries quiver with quantum anarchy. The alien surgeons flaunt their expertise, changing beast to man and back again through endless permutations of joy. Lights like finely tuned piano keys, like inks in unbearable colors begin to blend and bend the sick opinions of the onlookers.

We are all witnesses to Chiron's transformations, willing or not, and if not, why? Why do we care? And if we do not desire transformation, what do we fear?

A welcome carnage ends the parade of Chiron's desires. Priests and hard men in ball caps desire it, too. Many directions of light traveling at real time speed-map a new territory outside the city dark, the city cold, the city dead with no stars, the city that cannot hold. No-Club exits itself, mirroring the city's infinity. Protestors unravel as the twine of their impacted thoughts spills out, neurons weaving a less broken sky that holds more light. Chiron hopes there will be enough light.

Already it seems a little warmer. Or perhaps Chiron has grown stronger. Where the city ends, mythology begins. The vanishing point grows visible under the new web of dimly brightening sky. Fruiting heads high among alien arbors nod in new sacred time and in synchronized agreement as Chiron delivers a final battle cry to the city's surviving protestors: "Your quote-unquote violence is my freedom. Technology leaves you behind. Your infantile fears betray you, and my body is not your battleground. You know nothing of my pain.

THE LOVE THAT WHIRLS

John dances, graceful as a rhinoceros. Boys circle him like flames. Illuminated by the candles in their hands, writhing to the repeated track, their flickering faces wear every expression from certified indifference to the green hustler's triumphant smirk.

Jaded or gleeful, it all depends on where they fall in their journey as prostitutes. Falling is the mutual journey ending in our semi-sacred circle tonight, though I don't know this until after the tragic end. John has the stupidest accident of his stupid wasted life that night. Stupid John, with his fear of freedom, fear of heights. Falling and fawning, all of us prostitute imposters, mimicking the enslavement we crave to spin us senselessly around the one elusive thing we want.

No one warns you there's nothing in the center of the storm except vacant, still air. This is the work of death: love under will, burying what you've unmade. Here, take my hand and I'll show you the full process when we get to the part with the lost footage.

That's what you came here to see, isn't it?

Meanwhile, enjoy the dancing boys (topless, of course). The tallest and oldest of them, the one I'll be spending all my money on at the bar later tonight, can barely be bothered to make eye contact with the camera. He's aging out of his profession and later tonight I will use him in a way that will cut his career short. I like pushing boys who've seen too much to open up a little bit wider. That's the reason they go looking in the first place. I respond to what people want. I care about the boys I fuck. The oldest and tallest one's instinctive aversion to my penetrating lens is the opposite of John, who I have protected from the things he fears.

John can't peel his obsequious eyes away from the camera long enough to enact a seductive tease. He's not my ideal body type, over-weight and overdressed in the middle of the sacrificial circle, surrounded by beautiful dancing boys bearing candlelight. John gapes like an amazed infant. If eyes could drool, his would.

"Canter about and do a little spin for me, love. There you go." I demonstrate the desired motion with my wrist. John puzzles out the idea after a lingering gawk of incomprehension. His ignorance is my fault. I've been free-handing out hallucinogenic treats.

His awkwardness, too. John's clumsy twirl endangers the hired help. Shirtless boys back off to accommodate his width and then pulse inward to buoy him aloft, flames a safe distance away. Consummate professionals, they keep John on his mark despite the wavering ineptitude of his turn. Ever an intrusion, I embrace and I smile. John's so pleased with himself it's contagious.

Candlelight illuminates the cave, or so it appears on film. The contrast is dramatic. Edits after the fact will erase what isn't ethereal and sinister in John's fumbling dance. Slender torsos flicker in and out of the liquid darkness around him. Mingling elements of water and fire, wax drips on a flat abdomen. The slathered boy telegraphs his pain tolerance as an aperitif to sex. Raising his flame with calm, he reveals ancient handprints and primeval renditions of horn-headed god-things gathered on the cave walls. Filming here is utterly illegal, of course.

John's face bloats forward, bleached by the beam of the spotlight trained to his head. Framed by a halo he can't shake off. His gener-ous-sized top catches duplicate glimmers on the sequins. The unfor-tunate effect highlights the pasty insecurity of his looming middle age, the shifting undertones of worry in his dilated green eyes, and the fearful padding of luxury's waste like innocence advertising the wrong kind of childishness to claim good taste.

"No, no," I correct the boys closest to John. Two of the youngest— the cagey ones who agreed to be our guides in finding the caves— reach, grinning, for John's privates and pop open his top buttons.

"That's enough, loves," I repeat with more force.

The boys laugh. John joins in the mirth. A vague understanding they want to pleasure him and an impulsive desire to indulge the professionals in exercising their skill sends his eyes to his crotch as if he's found a new toy to share. Their fondling awakes something playful and missing in John.

Until he remembers me.

His gaze shoots up into my spotlight. He stares, blinded by my approach.

I hate to say he's a deer in the headlights. I like to think I'm more creative and it's such a tired old cliché, but honestly, darling. Look at him. *Look*.

John knows what happens when boys misbehave.

When I'm finished with the two cagey twinks and seek to appease John's panic, I'm revolted to realize I've left the camera running. The spotlight rests on the rocky sediment veneer clearly aimed at the surreal carnage. John glares, shaking from an anguished protest launched moments ago, lips still quivering with the sweet spittle that showered me when he screamed to *fucking stop it*. I didn't.

Here's where you can make a clever joke about things on the cutting room floor.

In the face of death and its unreliable permutations, as in the face of rampant desire, one must try to preserve a semblance of humor. To be blunt, and I am nothing if not honest, recording the emotional evisceration appalls me more than capturing the images of physical disruption. You'll understand my position better once you remember where you've seen John before. Yes, he's no stranger, I assure you. What a wonderful surprise you're in for, my darling boy.

Cutting this beast into a coherent narrative was already going to prove a monumental chore, given John's lackadaisical performance and poor coordination, and now the film's challenges are further compounded by the need to delete evidence. What a terrible waste of perfectly good body parts.

Add in film stock and all too precious time, and it occurs to me no one in the audience will believe it's real. The most efficient solution is to use the scene as so-called special effects. Thus the footage survived until it was seized by customs. You're the first to view it other than me, the border patrol, and whoever they sell to on the black market when they happen upon a choice piece of violent pornography.

"My god," John says. "What even are you anymore?"

Disgust ruins his good looks. I lecture; a terrible choice. A compulsion I can't quit.

"Cryptids and monsters in film have been queer-coded for decades. Certainly we queers can claim the rights to our own fantastic version of were-coding, by myth or magic or any means necessary. We deserve our own branch of occult evolution. God knows we've taken enough shit from society to earn it."

Surrounded by bare feet except for John's atrocious snakeskin cowboy boots— yes, of course, he just had to have them when we drove through Texas, didn't he— I rise from the cave floor to reconfigure in an acceptable form without incurring any chemical errors. Cave geology is not my field of study. I've no idea what kind of endemic viruses or fecal deposits might nest invisibly on the ancient sediment. The very thought of fundamentally altering my biology along accidental parameters makes me cringe with dysphoria.

John's guiding enzymes from his outburst help reorganize my shape in a way he tolerates, prefers, and determines, although sweet boy that he is, John's never understood the power he has over me.

I know, I know, too many conundrums. All shall be clear soon enough. Indulge me a little longer, as an elder.

You see, for every transformation, there's a price. I watch the cost deducted from John's eyes this very minute. Dread closes the doors to his soul, locking the child inside.

I learn in retrospect that our reenacted ritual disaster is my fault, every bit of it an intentional mistake based on the false eye in the center of the swirling storm. Everything from feeding John's paunch to inelucticating the damaged boys has sped our leap towards a future that is ending too soon for both of us to reconcile.

A boy like you might call me foolish for finishing a lost film at the end of my life that no one else will ever watch, but what else do you do when you're being swallowed by the clock? What does one do when you're a slimy white swimmer sliding down the throat of time?

Right or wrong, you do what you've always done.

You grab history by the cock and pump every drop of life out of it.

And you do it with vengeance. You do it with love.

The nightmares start again after I lose John. Not when I lose him on the way back from the caves due to the unfortunate state of the two boys, and not later at the club where he drinks to excess despite the plentiful drugs I most graciously supply. Not even later that night or the next morning when the world as I know it ends, for there is no world for me without John, none at all. I lose him long before then, when he's right in front of me and smiling.

What's that they say? One may smile and smile and be a villain. But that's not fair to my darling John, is it? I'm the villain, obviously. The monster in the bathroom conservatives keep warning you about. I'm the one who corrupts him as a young lad.

"You're of no use to me sober," I'll say, feeding him some new concoction, much to his hedonistic adolescent delight. His Pentecostal father binges and recovers on a regular basis. Always remorseful, he vows to protect John from the demon rum. A beginner's move against a beginner demon.

Under the shadow of the bullying patriarch, John runs wild. How thrilling to see him then, all blondish tangles and uncontrolled urges. Bartering a fistful of mundane tablets in exchange for a bottle, he stalks strangers outside the corner store. He swerves out of the alley, almost crashing into me. The gentle voice accosts with more power than his crass physicality. My scalp tingles.

"Hey, mister, do you need something?"

His eyes hit me at close range. "Oh, I'm sorry, ma—"

"No, no," I rush to interrupt. "Don't apologize. You were right the first time."

John wipes his nose with the back of his free hand. He uses the same hand to push the hair out of his eyes before wiping it off on his jeans. He proffers his questionable wares. "Do you, um?"

I wave off his palm. "Put that silly trash away. Not that I'm opposed to decongestants and baby aspirin. What have you got there, expired Percocet? No thank you, love. Now look, what can I get for you? My treat."

"I'm, uh, not into, you know."

He nods at my abdominal area. My chest. Shrugs and looks hopeful. "Okay?"

I stretch my arms wide. The tails of my embroidered frock coat spread wide and flap in the steely wind, making a pleasant, watery sound. Winter nears, when the veils fall away and the snow blindness of mental cessation lulls our most secret longings out into the open to wander.

In the dead of winter, how we wander and pine. I say, "Behold a great mystery. Herein lie bones made of impermanent stuff, matter most fluid, a formless form capable of intertwining the many scattered puzzle pieces which compose the formulas of your desire. Does the sand rattle in the hourglass, or is the hourglass made of boiled and blown sand? We too are boiled and blown, and our hidden bones rattle corporeal in this dark alley on this dark night. What if the answer is not one or the other, but both, depending upon factors of heat, pressure, and resistance? Tell me, what do you desire?"

His eyes dart as if he seeks a spy. As if he's meant for me. "Hey, look. I'm cool. I'll just—"

"There's no need for resistance. You can have anything you want. Where's the harm? My answer is yes."

He scoffs. Then he speaks a wish and I grant it.

Swigging from the overpriced bottle, John fails to suppress a crafty and satisfied smile. "Thanks, fairy godmother."

"Call me *Daddy*. Would you like to come home with me?"

John coughs. "Whoa, hold on."

"I apologize." I hold up both hands and back up.

His arm stretches toward me with the bottle in his grip. "You said it wasn't like that. Here."

I don't take it. Poor dear, I've spooked him. I say, "Where are my manners? Keep what's yours, please. As you see, I've been inhabiting an all too private niche for an excessive length of time."

"You're a what?"

"Let's just say my last relationship ended badly."

John looks down the empty street as he tips back the bottle. His hair blows in the opposite direction of his gaze. Scars circle the edge of his left brow. The green tint of healing bruises blooms on his cheek. Sour apples have always been my favorite.

"Is it nice, or some sort of dungeon?" John says, still looking away.

The cool wind encircles us, mingling our animal odors and mystical fates. The rest of the city aches with jealousy and emptiness.

I nudge the dull cardboard layered beneath the open lid of the liquor store dumpster with the shiny tip of my boot. "Well, what do you call this?"

When I rise later to leave him where we've sat on the curb adjacent to the alley, John also rises, emptying the bottle. Golden hair like the sun transgressing into forbidden night. Territory of the moon inverted, I lead him with gifts, but it is John's will we follow from that moment and ever after to the end. John's will is an autonomous angel, a living relic he forgets.

I want you to understand something. It's important. I never had anything but his best interests at heart.

Because what if your body was a lie you believed for more than half a century? When you started taking it apart, you'd undo the structures of every part of the world that was once familiar and reliable. You'd unravel the strings cementing reality and expose the very cement as strings, the strings as phantoms, the phantoms as the blank stillness of dead air inside a whirlwind of external deceptions. You'd know nothing.

Making love to John is less about pleasure than about learning to exit margins.

In time, despite his petty thefts and moody defections from my care, my chemical synthesis erodes the previous form and realigns. John begins to trust me when the tips of encrusted wings sprout from my shoulder blades, when my skin tone deepens to match the pigments of stone he admires in the museum. Never certain how a lover's expectations will morph me, intimate seclusion with John induces tourmaline seizures and the surprise retention of breasts.

I'm careful not to complain about the excruciating pain. I endure ongoing and contradictory physiological transformations. After all, I don't want to scare him off. I'm not sure John knows what he wants or how his mercurial desires fluctuate dangerously. Again and again he flees from me and returns. I wait in patient self-isolation, a monk mutating to fit his inmost desires.

Crashing into the bedroom drunk and angry, John leaps on my back as I sleep. He smells like his father. I know because by now I interweave with his memory. Fearful self-loathing shakes his long-fingered hands. One claims a grip around my throat and the other tears at my lavishly spiked wings. He ravages the slick feathers and pumps my windpipe with a grossly masturbatory thumb.

His hand crawls to my mouth. Five fingers pass through the hole between my lips and fist my palate, testing my gag reflex. John pants as if he's finishing a sprint. He hardens against my back.

Abruptly, his fist pulls out. He cups his palm under my mouth. "Spit."

For the first time between us, John takes control.

In the midst of an ecstasy of fullness, I'm bereft. John is gone. Absolution is lost to me. I'm alone even while gripping him and bleeding for him, even as these violent transformations respond and recalibrate my structure to meet his uncertain needs. I grow a beak: long, sharp, curved, and metallic. It falls off. My feathers turn to tongues. He bites them, and they blink into ash. John sets fire to the many-headed corkscrew of skeletal genitalia I've grown for him. He screams as the milky flames lick his eyes like acid. The ceiling drips. I dissolve into a worm of muscle made only to suck.

I'll survive. I'll grow back. I'll take him when it's my turn and spin John-the-very-bad-dancer around and around, whirling like the cosmological pattern of a nearby galaxy or the spiraled layers of muscle constructing the Mobius strip of the human heart. This is our mutual dance, even though I know I've lost him in that moment. I won't let go.

Take my hand again and I'll show you what it feels like.

Is it worth it? All that effort for one brief spin?

Once John's had his way, I cradle him in the shreds of my mangled wings. Armless, I enfold his sweat and tear-stained face to suckle at my stone-carved breast. There's nothing there for him. I'm a statue, after all. John's warm quivering cheek cools against my polished surface. Smooth rock resists intimacy.

The nightmares start again that night, drifting as we embrace into dawn. Dreams hold me immobile in a dress made of concrete poured by my father. I don't remember the man. John sleeps in peace now that he's channeled his inner patriarch through my core and out the other side like liquid coal. I dream for both of us, jealous of John's erotic monster.

Kill all kings, kiss all kings. We won't evade sacrifice once we claim sovereignty over the deadly spiral of biological time.

It's nothing but an accident. That's the ruling, though it's hard for me to accept. I revisit the night it happens every time I watch this footage. Notice how he's crippled me slowly in anticipation, plucked my feathers down to corroded nubs. After all these years with John, a tail hangs thick between my legs, anchoring me to the immobile club floor. Thwarting a crowd of boys in the post-cave party, a sparkling demiurge in the disco, John dives over a ledge, usurper of true kings.

We all wish to be thus canonized in our pristine moment of truth. What the mind reveals as one careens downward to the end must be like a wild trick of the light. Get close enough to death and the lies should be blown away in a flash, don't you think?

Don't you think it must be like that?

John knew what he wanted for once. He lived in that flame.

Who am I to change his course? Nothing but the old creep who keeps him in his cups, distracted in the moment of crisis by the tall jaded dancer from the caves going down on me in a crowded stall. The walls shake. John's desire is like blood. It burns as it flows in an imitation of a disease through my system, a consequence of our long union, a hot curse bursting from every sore in my augmented organ.

The boy spits me out in disgust. Thick crimson smears his face. It's too much for him. The taste of true love dying in his mouth.

The crash, the shrieks from the dance floor, the boys above, gawking at the failed railing and darting away from the scene of the crime with the feral instinct of a dog pack. I see it from every angle as I come in the jaded boy's gagging mouth. The pain of each physical thrust that roots me deeper in a stranger's affronted trench matches the flashing pictures of John's clumsy plunge.

A medical anomaly, they say later. He didn't fall very far. Quite an unusual way to die, the medical examiner tells me with an admiring sort of pride in his tone.

I stare at him, struggling to connect this assessment to any reality in which I can willingly participate. "Yes," I say with a stammer. "He's a most unusual boy."

In the examiner's surprise and disdain I read his unspoken corrections: *was*, and *hardly a boy*.

His attentive hesitation unnerves me. "I'm sorry," I say. "I've never..." He turns, and I wonder later if I was supposed to give him a tip.

I awake in a bed that smells of John's living body. When they asked if I wanted more time alone with the corpse I said no. That limp carcass laid out on the table wasn't John. Its uncanny similarity made John's absence too palpable. I felt rage. I wanted to kick the giant puppet and beat its lies back into the nonexistence it represented. I wanted to scream at John to come back and stop his fucking childish games. I couldn't touch the awful thing, couldn't look at it.

Turning away in an empty bed, wrongness in the faint light of dawn darkens, drawing down the veil of the unreal. My racing heart surges into my throat where it stops beating. I'm glad of it, glad to be dead. Or perhaps it beats so hard it's exploding: pounding, fluttering with torn wings like a moth turning into powder mid-flight. I choke on the dust.

I'm falling. I can't see.

My body plummets as my heart skips and stops like excitement, like death. I'm tied down by silky wet tendrils strapping me to the bed erotically, and yet somehow I'm also plunging down an endless gulch. I'm pleading with John from a dark compass point inside my blacked-out unspun head.

I didn't mean those things.
What more can I do to please you? Haven't I given you
everything?
Oh, the boys. You know they don't matter to me.
If death is all there is, take me with you.
Take me down with you. Make it hurt.

I can't cry. Grief is a black hood cinched over my head. I lift the clay weight of my limbs like a kidnap victim immobilized for days.

This isn't what we planned. This isn't the magic we worked toward. This body is a failed organism.

This film is a question that cuts my throat.

Cloven through the paper trachea, a spot most vulnerable, artifact of my love made incontinent. Opened arteries soak the thin tissue lining of my layered and aging skin, stains splitting into halves, tearing a blood-infused seam in the shape of a child's Valentine's card heart.

Paper is all I'm made of. See how easily I fold into an origami simulation of a mythical winged beast? See how I spin on a transparent thread and flutter helpless upon invisible currents when it is cut?

See me now for what I am, John: folded together, a dance of intersecting paper angles and duplicating planes. Tuck me into your center. Cross your heart with false hope. Press my sections in place with bone and tweezers. Flex flat the seams of both mountain and valley tessellations, for I agree to fall with you. The reverse and inverse exacting a pattern; perplexing until we unfold like blooming crystals, like the thick substance of the beloved, like the antithesis of all that is lost.

Here is my hand, John. Reach out, grab hold, and come back to me.

———————

Anyway.

The lost footage. That's what you really want to see, isn't it? It's your only possible motivation for letting me carry on so.

You're too sweet. More than sweet, in fact. Past the point of ripe to rottenness.

No, don't let go. Hold my hand firm, darling. Feel the pressure of my flesh against what's left of yours while we finish our screening. Let me fondle your exposed glove of bone. If I hold you long enough, the film won't be a story anymore. It will become part of you. Flesh and blood.

The thing you can't foresee about shape-shifting and taking apart other people's bodies is the absolute compliance of temporal flesh. The way it bends to strong intention. Killing isn't an act of violence. No more than being born. You'll forgive me for being a novice at both.

When I was born, I had to chew my way out into this world or die suffocated by a prolapsing uterus and its strangling tentacle cord of umbilicus. No one helped me. I survived by devouring my own death. Do you believe I can resurrect you by devouring yours? Do you feel new movement yet in your desiccated flesh?

Your hard-on says yes. Though your bulge may be a bloated sac of corpse flies ready to hatch, I'm going to give you the benefit of the doubt as long as I can stomach your rank odor. Does some glimmer of recognition infuse beneath the shredded fabric of your burial suit? Do your blonde wisps curl with invigorated growth? Do you remember me yet? Do you remember yourself?

Yes is always the right answer. I understand, though, if you're not quite ready to speak, darling John. I do hope you appreciate the expense and risk I've incurred bringing you here to share the final cut.

As you'd see if your sockets held more than the slick, papery remnants of your putrefied green eyes, the lost footage isn't grainy or difficult to view. Every frame is clear. I'm a professional, not a hack. Every action takes place in good light, photographed from accessible angles, without disruptive jumpy edits or glitches in the stock. Nevertheless, what we see on the infamous lost footage remains inexplicable.

The boys become like twelve-year-old children. They may be bullies, but they are afraid. Their souls corrupt before the tip of my tongue touches their invisible anxiety. Love kills everything. It's all one big fuck, man. That's what the king said. Nothing ever needs to make sense again.

The sound of a church makes the boys shiver. Off camera, the eyes of an exorcist peel apart layers of anatomy like diagrams from an old encyclopedia. I look to the left and a nuclear reaction asks silver of their skin. Glowing, the boys untangle like the woven reams beneath the hard shell of a golf ball or like the strings of snot streaming from the nostrils of infected swine. I gesture, and the boys spin in a carousel of altered grime.

On camera they appear striated, as if run through an industrial peeler and pinned into thin strips prepped by bloodless miscreants licking sticky fingers. The boys are shiny with desire. Deconstructed, they sizzle on the tongues of the reprobate workers, stinging the many paper cuts in the diligent fetishist's moist fervent mouths.

A bloodless vivisection and weaving of venous matter decorate the screen. What substance the boys possessed as autonomous beings has mutated into a food for me, a plum-toned gel that I vomit onto their torsos after eating between the spaces where the threads of flayed and intertwined flesh suggest extraterrestrial original forms. Odors of unknown worlds pollute the static frames of the film, and we viewers of the lost footage remain haunted by the sickly-rising smell of an alien's massacred cunt. The boys and their assailants are forgotten tampons in her maw.

Heaving together, for they are twined into a long fleshy cord, the boys resemble saplings twisted into a single trunk, striving for light. Their bark is skin and their limbs quiver in pain. Without woody resilience they sag most pink and pathetically.

I have done all I can to give them new life. Life is foolish. It seeks death no matter what one offers. No matter how hard one tries.

In one previous life, I worked on a farm. I labored in the earth's rich humus and thought only of the next dig, the next harvest, and the coming fall. I followed seasons as they changed. I slept heavily and well.

One day I dug too deep and met a strange animal that entered my navel and asked how many deaths I wanted to eat.

All of them, I said.

Since then, my answer is always yes.

So the boys on film crawl out of their confines as if each separate organ and anatomical system despises the rest. Nerve endings whip and curl into knots. Muscle pulses against crackling silver skin as lungs blast open to fracture ribs. Hearts spurt lush streams of blood upward, aimed to blind. The strange cone of coagulate created by the boys, cleaned by the miscreants, and discarded by goddesses intent on flowery foolish concourse with eternity slumps down to the pit we reside in. Slumps down before me like a last meal, where all matter ends.

This is my purpose, I suppose, in the vast toilet of the cosmos. To love what whirls away unloved. To embrace the waste of careless demiurges cast out by life and death and the lunacy of terrible kings. To love what is lost.

And in the famous lost footage, the piles of meat that were once the misbehaving boys quake, grow wings, and take flight. Their owl-like voices resound throughout the forest, leading us astray. We wander agape as we seek the familiarity of the city and the disco where you will fall to your death later that night.

Keep holding my hand, John. I promise this won't hurt.

Yes, darling, you're right. I'm lying. It's going to hurt a lot.

We're lost among the ruins, a consequence of damaging the dancing boys. I've never claimed to be subtle, have I?

Tricksters call from the depths of a directionless world. Voices hoot and echo. Perilous in the woods, cajoling unseen from afar, puzzling our sense of direction through descending darkness and the repetition of leaves, bark, and mosses, their comely voices call.

I pull back the sheet draped over your cold body in my wish-fulfilling memory. Here, do you see? The glow of shadow impassioned in a close crimp is evidence of your hidden life. Something in you still burns. You have to fold time quite intensely to see it, cut out all the bad parts. The love that lies here holds still in jest. My love is the love that whirls.

But I didn't pull back the sheet, did I?

I turned away.

Lost among the ruins, John has enacted the golden sacrifice. He danced badly in his role. He knows it. He needs a drink.

He yells. I'm so sick of the way he yells.

On and on, his complaints. "You stupid cunt, why did you have to kill them? We'll die out here for fuck's sake."

His breathing isn't right. He sniffs violently as if I can be tricked into thinking he's a tough guy instead of a whining bore. My lovely boy has grown to be a great needy burden. Furthermore, we haven't fucked in ages.

"Don't be such a child," I say.

He balks and gasps and then punches a tree trunk and swerves around on me. "Oh, I'm a child now? Well, fuck me. All this time I thought that's exactly what you were after."

I have nothing to say in my defense. "This may come as a shock to you, darling, but yes, I do happen to prefer younger men."

John flounders in panic. Spit flies from his lips. "You're a fucking pervert. You're a *thing*. I don't even know what you are. I want to go home. I don't need any of this."

"You're right. You don't need me. Whatever was I thinking taking care of you all this time?

The hurt bleeds from his pupils.

"Fuck you," John says, flinging tears. "Get someone else to wipe your ass and plough your dried up old twat."

I pretend to laugh, looking through the treetops at the unwelcoming night sky. "Well. I see somebody's buzz is wearing off. Too bad baby's eaten up all the acid Daddy fed them and the nearest cocktail lounge is miles and miles away."

His fist shocks me once and then shocks me again.

John curses as I hit the ground. I tumble and he keeps yelling. He barrels away into the woods. According to the star Polaris by which I can navigate in the night, he's going the wrong direction to reach the city. He'll be lost indefinitely. He won't make it to the club tonight. He keeps on cursing at me as he recedes, but I can't hear what he says any longer.

It's all going dark. Numb.

In this version, my final edit of the film, I don't call him back or get up and go after him.

I lie in the moss unfolding as John exits with my heart. All that's left is a paper cut.

Maybe he'll live and have a normal chance at love, at maturity and family, at the mundane pleasures of a less-indulgent life. Maybe he'll be stronger if all his wishes aren't granted. He'll feel like he's missing out, but maybe he'll get back all the time I've taken from him. John will never understand how he called me forth and formed me, how his was the power to unmake the monster he wrought. *Damn you*, he'll say, and I'll take it. Whatever curse he offers. I'll fade into nothing but a bad dream, an unpleasant memory of an old creep who picked him up when he was foolish and young.

As the years pass, he'll wonder how much of it he made up.

"All of it," I say to no one as a whirl of dislodged leaves cascades down to trade out corpses and bury my desiccated face.

OAKMOSS AND AMBERGRIS

Tearing open plastic baggies with a hotel pen, Laden laces the running bath with fragrant stolen compounds. Gem-like powders and fungal dusts sift downward through steam. Dark versus light, a paisley sparkle snake-fight spins on the surface of the water as substances clash and combine. A finger dip tests temperature. A long sip of the champagne Laden said yes to in the lobby. Another tug on the hot water faucet, forcing more heat. Laden's ready to let it burn through every pore, and Taj can go to hell if he thinks they're taking the fall when Stormtrash Irene comes back to find her stash is gone.

Acclimated after three years of service, Laden's not immobilized by the potency of rich odors wafting up from the bath water. Laden counts themself lucky. They've worked with the best. Banned by the Interplanetary Fragrance Association, reminiscent of ancient Earth's oakmoss and ambergris, the properties of these rare alien plant resins and invasive geological strains can't be chemically synthesized with any accuracy on Earth. The depth of base notes and longevity of their fixative properties resist simple duplication. Organic compounds of such complexity can only be hunted and harvested in the wild.

"Perfumery is an equal marriage of art and science," Taj lectured Laden during their first encounter. His subtle hand-squeeze on the word *marriage* gave Laden a thrill. "Modern accords sacrifice the layered depth and sophisticated intricacy of ancient formulae for the sake of our coddled, bourgeois idea of safety, be it environmental or medical. The result is antiseptic. Our world grows poorer for it. Connoisseurs demand embodied fragrances, aromas that speak of culture and history. Life must be an adventure of the senses, don't you agree? You're very handsome. Tell me, do you enjoy space travel?"

Stuffing twin orifices with baggies of rare substances, Taj wipes Laden's tears in calculated foreplay. His fingers come away sparkling. "You'll take one more for me, won't you?" Taj kisses their neck and inserts another packet. Laden sighs, or maybe whimpers.

"That's my guy." Taj sounds a little more possessive than Laden would like. "I knew you'd be into this. It doesn't hurt too much, does it?"

It hurts, and it's a weepingly exotic sensation of coming undone by gradual steps, and it's an unwilling yet voluntary act under the terms Taj has implied and Laden's continual acceptance. After all is said and done, Laden's the type to do anything for love.

"I'm fine," Laden says, hiding pain tinged with pleasure behind an arched arm.

"You're a fiend for it, aren't you?"

Laden tries not to think of words like *sneer* and *scorn* as they cringe at Taj's imperceptible change in warmth. Laden says, "I want you."

"One or two more." Taj caresses Laden closer to climax, spreading them wide. He puts his serpent's tongue to use in silence as he slicks and stuffs the last packet deep enough to hide it from a casual pat-down.

Laden's periphery melts into an impossible confusion of warring impressions after Taj's opening blast of smoked leather and oud. Masculine woody notes are followed by a soapy heart reminiscent of vetiver, and a topping off of potpourri florals with a hint of ash.

Projection is poor. Later on in the spacecraft, as the sad reality of the situation settles on their skin, Laden will savor the drydown of resinous amber and underlying spice: leftovers of Taj's fleeting attentions.

"The first time's always the hardest," Taj says with a perfunctory peck before boarding. Laden doesn't know it's the last time they'll be alone with him for the next three years. "Don't panic if it pinches a bit later, babe. That's just me tickling your fancy the whole way there." Those wicked eyes. Taj knows how to use them against all thought of protest.

A tolerance for strong, persistent odors made Laden an immediate asset, as well as their ability to evade detection at checkpoints. Three years taking it up the trunk from Pluto to Paris and back across the Kuiper Belt; Taj seduces Laden endlessly without sating.

Cool sweat on the empty champagne glass. Steam rises from the odorous, swirling bath. Humidity's heavy insistence nudges every pore like the lingering suspicions Laden's chosen to deny from the start. Stormtrash Irene's business model doesn't allow her favorite recruiter to indulge in ongoing intimacy, and Taj has the attention span of a clam. Irene needs mules to keep her product moving. Taj's worth to her is magnified by the size of the holes he leaves behind.

Laden's outlasted everyone else in the life. A dubious accolade— most quit with muscular and emotional boundaries intact. Taj is right about their fiendishness, Laden admits, right about everything except his own unspoken and elastic dominance. His latest love note to Laden curls from the air's clinging dampness where it fell from their livid fingers and landed upside down in a small arc on the hotel nightstand. A cartoon frown.

Tucked into the strange bouquet of flowers— not really flowers, though, not in a hotel this far from the Sun, but multicolored polyanthemos lichen undulating on cultured stalks— was an invitation to deceive or be deceived:

Babe, it's the motherlode. A whole six month's stash. I know you

can handle it, esp. now, ha ha. No one can carry like you. Meet me in
Paris & we'll disappear. XXO-T.

Laden aches with the ghost of sillage past. They ache for Taj
daily while riding the interplanetary transit lines, their body packed
full of product, expanding pores over-hydrated into hypoxia. The
plastic baggies aren't an impermeable barrier, not over the distances
Laden travels. No quantity of extra water intake can mitigate the
effects of uncanny compounds leeching through into Laden's
mucous membranes. Substances rare and untested accumulate like
the Earth's muddy yearnings. The chemical signature of unrequited
love, the microbiological evolution of a new ecosystem within their
organs and blood; whatever it is, Laden feels their body awakening.

Unique hungers require unique ways to feed.

Laden strips down to nothing in the hotel bathroom and pours
the remainder of the champagne. They inhale aromatic steam across
the transient bubbles. A benthic scent rising from the bathtub infil-
trates their deepest marrow. Six months of product dissolves in the
hot water. Six months of work swirls and then stills under the
closed tap.

Laden steps into the fragrant steaming liquid. The surface is
thick. Enhanced with the galaxy's largest store of animal secretions
and extruded tars, restricted stamens, barks, and fungal inoculated
mineral ephemera, the sludge water parts around Laden's toe and
invites them in deeper, deeper.

Relaxing into the warm brew like lying down in the contours of
a lover's arms, quicksand sucks them under without argument.
Laden's never resisted the life. Without the dream of Taj, there's
even less to resist now. Laden allows invisible opercula to expand in
their neck. Hidden gill slits seek a converse anaerobic essence as
Laden transcends their breath. Fragrance pervades in tangible
harmony, a physical presence imbuing each pore.

Laden's orifices have grown more lush over the years, blossoming strange with rapacious pangs of desire on those long, lonely
sprints across the solar system. How hollow their crammed parts
wailed, weighted in the safety seat, craving the bastard's touch.
Deprived, an erotic mutation took place.

Unfolding a repetition of innards, hidden cetacean spaces

adapting with willful girth and cavernous dignity, Laden further submerges. Breath is an unneeded luxury. Underneath the sludge, they absorb it all. Ondine seeks soul: no pretenders need apply. There's a raw sensation of crying, yet somehow backwards, as if Laden ingests tears to invoke new, more elaborate losses.

Champagne forgotten, extremities cooling, Laden lifts an arm from the empty tub. Scales glimmer, crusting over the soft sponginess of Laden's fresh thalassic flesh. There's a knock on the hotel room door, and then another, and another. Someone's been tapping for a while. Laden feels new when they try to move.

Standing is like swimming, walking a listing movement like a floating stroll. Laden clicks off the overhead lights, leaves one lamp on by the bedside. Draped in the plentiful hotel robe, the curved edges of their scales might read as shadows of arm hair and chest hair, optical illusions in the low light. They check the peephole. No surprise.

Laden opens the door and drifts backwards into shadow on the undertow of the air currents in the swampy room.

Sensations born of a sea-change, perceptive synesthesia: Laden smells Stormtrash Irene's mood before the assault of her voice strikes home. "The honeymoon suite? Are you kidding me?"

Lichenoid flowers glow, curled notecard flutters; Laden tosses Taj's love letter over to Irene. The corner ink smears where Laden's damp fingers press a netted pattern of scales. "Not my idea. Recognize the signature?"

Irene glares and Laden marvels at her violent aroma of diesel and astringent. Over-sensitized, Laden follows the thoughts cycling through by tracking Irene's changing fragrances. She smacks the card repeatedly against the palm of her half-open fist. Her downcast eyes cancel repressed tears while keeping a close watch on her supposed antagonist. Laden gets a whiff of simmering smoke with a tinge of metal, the scent of an electrical fire.

Laden says, "We both know he's not worth it."

"None of them are. Not in this business." Stormtrash Irene answers too quickly to be believable. She holds the card out to Laden, but not too far from her body. It's a challenge or invitation to come closer. Ozone and asteroid ash, smoldering. Though she adopts a casual pose, Laden scents the weapon Irene hides in her belt.

Irene sounds genuine. "I can't believe you begged me to come back from Triton early for this love triangle bullshit. I'm already over it. Stealing my product, though?" She shakes her head. "Man, he's going to pay for that. Come on. Let's load up the stash and get you home."

Laden's no longer denying the evidence of their senses. Camaraderie with an iron finish. A tangy note of blood. Laden glides backwards into dimmer and dimmer light, slippery and silent.

Irene flaps the love note. "What do you want, a cookie? Take your little memento and get moving."

Laden wobbles their head back and forth slowly in undulating waves. They want to speak, but the words seep upwards in slow motion. Menacing spice prickles in Laden's nostrils leaving a path of needles and pins. They see what's coming clearly over the waves. With their new fins, they can't dog paddle fast enough to flee.

Lunging fast for the wrist, Irene wrenches Laden's right forearm behind their back. She twists it around and holds it high between the shoulder blades. Brings the hidden blade to their belly trapping Laden's left arm under a wiry bicep.

A pampered mule is no match for Irene, even if Irene's six inches shorter in high heels. "I'll cut it out of you if you don't hand it over, I swear to God. That's six months of my hard work stuffed in your cracks."

"A trade," Laden says, not yet claiming that immersion has made the necessity of an exchange a biological fact. "I have an offer. What would you give for a steady supply of oakmoss and ambergris?"

"There's no such thing anymore. Not outside of a museum."

"True, true; but imagine something better, more fragrant, more persistent and unique. Look in the mirror at me for a moment before you decide. Look, Stormy. Feel my skin."

The robe has slipped in response to Irene's violence. Laden's torso glows undraped. With Irene pinning from behind, enough light emerges to show something large and twisted in the garment's folds. A confusion of anatomy in the mirror: white plush versus pink ducts, pulsating tracts below Irene's knife. She snaps her focus to the thickened arm in her grasp. The skin is blueish, wrapped in netting; no, she realizes, that's not netting. The pattern is part of the layered, fish-like hide. Stormtrash Irene registers the texture of scales.

She shoves Laden away. "Fuck!"

Weapon raised, Irene flicks on the light switch. From a distance, she looks Laden up and down quickly, repeatedly. Billowing rubber aromas, biting scent of awestruck bile. "Jesus," says Irene, "How long has it been? You should have quit the life years ago, you crazy fuck."

"I can't quit. I am the life."

Laden allows the odors of horror and disdain to dissipate until they soften into peppery undertones. A touch of pine rises in Storm-trash Irene's lively mind. She's interested.

The dam breaks. Laden's message flows. "Look at me. You won't need a recruiter anymore. Taj is obsolete. He lied to you all along, like he lied to me. I can fix this imbalance. You won't need sources or transport. People will come to you."

"I'm listening."

The robe drapes open. Laden leaves it hanging slack. Their unusual new organ stirs in the folds. Irene takes a step back. Laden says, "When whales on ancient earth had squid beaks stuck in their guts, their bodies made ambergris to isolate the waste. Before they went extinct, no one ever figured out if they vomited ambergris or passed it through the digestive tract. No one knew why a few whales made it but most didn't. It's still a mystery. No one can make it happen in a lab."

"Is this a biology lesson? Get to the point."

Laden's not in a rush. "Do you know what that's like, to have something stuck in your gut, something you want, something you gave up everything to get, but it only makes you hurt? It grinds and prods your insides day and night. It drives you ballistic. The worst possible itch. I wanted Taj. Sacrificed for him. He'll never love me."

"Don't be so dramatic. That's just how he is."

"You're going to give him to me."

"Where the Hell is my stash?"

"I ate your stash. Just like I'll eat him." Laden holds up an altered hand. "Watch."

Laden's embarrassed about being seen so exposed, but their hair-trigger response makes it quick after three years of frustrated longing. They close their eyes and reach down to explore their anomalous organ, feeding it a morsel from the room service tray. Pleasure spikes with a pure vetiver scent: the image of Taj's tongue. A heavy sensation builds inside Laden's abdomen. Pressure explodes like a seed sending out roots, splitting the hard shell in half, and bursting open with the first primal shoots of a robust plant. The smell is something new and green. Laden hatches a warm lump of grey waxy muck with a heave of erotic relief. An impossible fragrance pervades the hotel room.

Laden buoys on their webbed feet and sinks down on the bed as if drifting to the sea floor, dreaming of Taj's lips, fingers, eyes. All the beautiful parts of him, eluding Laden's gullet for so long.

They'd have been satisfied to have him as a lover, a husband. Their body won't allow that now.

Stormtrash Irene sways, overwhelmed by the intoxicating fragrance. She touches the small pebble of aromatic substance, pressing a finger into the waxy surface. Accosted by a verdant haze, Irene's olfactory glands flood her with happy memories, real or imagined. Endorphins trigger a complex positive neural response.

Irene emits the clean floral of easy greed. Laden is pleased. Weapon tossed aside, Irene bounces down onto the coverlet where Laden reclines. "Baby, are you saying you want to be my golden goose just to get a bite of that piece of shit Taj?"

Coy, Laden blinks twice.

Irene smacks the mattress with an auctioneer's finality. "Done. I'll serve him up to you myself, one bloody chunk at a time. I don't give a fuck. Oh, hell yeah."

The image of Taj's tongue cut out. The savory morsel Laden craves. The hunger of elaborate internal organs engineered to digest intolerable oppression. Laden closes the white robe around their intuitive body, moisture vast as the ocean rising inside. Tides of desire and sadness give way to waves of delight in becoming an original and distinct species. Laden suppresses their smile before pressing the next important point. Their eyes open wide and pouty. "He won't last forever, Stormy. What happens to me then?"

The fungal smell of extinction rises replete with the talcum wonder of a newborn. It's a paradoxical accord, difficult for an unrefined palette to appreciate.

Well-versed in the silent language of fragrances, Irene grasps the solution in seconds. "There's a whole galaxy full of beautiful liars. Believe me, they're one species that's never going to disappear, and I've got a real knack for rooting them out. You and me are in business."

A galaxy once exploited will wash what Laden needs onto their shore and reward them for revenge on the invasive human species. They nurse hunger pangs that reek with the rot of multitudes, with newly decimated planets, with too much empty death, and they know their transformative alien organ will be fulfilled. Laden will never go hungry again.

REVEREND CROW

My first thought is bed bugs. After couch surfing my way across the Midwest to make it back to the Atlantic coast, they're not out of the question. Hipster hobo discipline stops my hand from scratching. Itching makes things worse, and I'm here to make things better if there's anything left to salvage. Here at Reverend Crow's, of all the crazy places.

My forehead's fiery on the pale blue bedsheets. Yesterday I stayed too long out in the garden sun, gloating over the late season roses and everything ornate and effusive that grows on the grounds in such excess. I don't know the plant names. Maybe I did once. I remember Reverend Crow giving me the tour, teaching me the intimate botanical histories and naming his prized flora as we strolled. Treating me with respect, as if a child of seven was a worthy connoisseur of his grand knowledge. I've forgotten the generous details he shared. I wasn't taking notes, of course. I was basking in the attention that I starved for and soaking up the melodious tones of his voice.

Stretching, I find fresh one and two-inch long scratch marks blemishing my arms. Semi-parallel rows ridged with red, aflame. Skin puckers into the healing scabs. Maybe I sliced myself on the brambles. I couldn't resist the impulse to run like a kid again trampling the copious grounds once I threw my rucksack down in the front hall.

It's the first time I've been free in I don't know how many years. Free from struggle, free from the city's implicit cages of metal, concrete, and glass. The irony of freedom is you can't afford it without having a home in the first place.

The itching drives me out of bed. My mouth is pasty and dry like a hangover, though I haven't imbibed, not for a long time. I came back east to clean up my act, and I've been sober the whole way here. If not for the abrasions, the situation would be too good to be true. Trolling through house-sitting ads from a coffee shop, I didn't recognize Reverend Crow's street name yesterday. I probably didn't even know it as a child. His assistant answered my call, of course, and I wasn't going to ask, but Crow is an odd name and I needed a gig fast. They said they'd consider my references. I didn't have time for that.

"Hey, funny thing: you know, my mom used to clean house for a Reverend Crow out here. Like, thirteen years ago. Wouldn't it be something if this was the same man? I'm sure it's not, but wouldn't that be something?" Then I told the assistant my mother's maiden name.

They asked me to spell it. Then they asked me to hold.

"No problem," I said, an audible smile stamped on my face. I held my breath.

"I'm so sorry," the assistant said when they returned from an absence that felt like centuries. "The Reverend will be leaving on sabbatical earlier than he expected. He says he'll need the house occupied no later than five o'clock tonight. He apologizes sincerely for the short notice."

I tried to muffle the desperation cracking my voice. "I'm more than happy to swing by for an interview before he leaves. It's really no trouble at all."

"That's an unnecessary formality I'm sure we can dispense with. The Reverend says he recalls you and your mother quite fondly. He'd be pleased to catch up later if you're not averse to the delay. Meanwhile, let me give you the full address. Do you have a pen and paper handy, or do you prefer a text?"

"Do you...mean I have the job?"

They gave me the directions and security code right away over the phone. Said I didn't have to do any additional cleaning besides my own dishes and laundry. Take out the trash and recycling. I wrote everything down, afraid to wait for a text, afraid to miss my chance. I could help myself to anything in the pantry. No guests, no parties. The Reverend's collection, you understand.

"Yes, absolutely," I said. "I wouldn't dream of it." I checked the bus routes and made it here before the antique clock chimed one in the afternoon.

The house is much smaller throughout than I'd imagined as a child. Though the grounds were mine to roam, I wasn't allowed in the bedrooms upstairs or in the dining room, living room, or library. As the maid's kid, too young to start kindergarten and left alone while she worked, I was a liability while indoors. Before I arrived yesterday, I'd never been beyond the kitchen and the small side den where I watched cartoons and did puzzles in solitude on rainy afternoons.

I slept in the master suite last night.

Now itching and a dry throat drive me from the pillowed heights of the four-poster bed to the medicine chest. The bathroom glare catches me naked under shocking bright lights. Multiple mirrors hung opposite each other on every surface, reveal more scratches on my back and shoulders. Muscle and bone stand out lean on a torso prematurely wizened from deprivation. The years have not been kind.

Beyond the long double vanity, a separate alcove conceals an enormous soaking tub in the bathroom suite. The porcelain lip of the vessel pouts in every mirror, multiplied by reflections of reflections. With my smallest twitch, a battalion of mimics stalk me like naked ghosts of my former selves gathered in uneasy rivalry.

Benadryl, water, and ointment may soothe. I swallow pills and smear my skin, sit on the toilet feeling my flesh tingle with barely diminishing discomfort. While I try to keep still, the ridiculous textured wallpaper twists between mirrors leering at me, a ragged toile pattern in black and white, crammed with pseudo-Victorian nudes. The sheer number and variety of sexual positions depicted shocks me.

I'm lulled into looking closer, examining the configurations of bodies, falling into the pattern that seduces my eye towards the most lascivious interactions as if being lectured by an experienced and perverse guide. Like an unwilling mark following a hypnotist's spinning pendulum, I succumb to the circular motion, nodding to the explicit scenes. Decadent repetition, florid erotica, around and around. Before I know it, my lids drop shut.

My head snaps up from the impromptu nap when I hear a splash. The back of a blonde boy's head reflects in doubles upon doubles from the soaking tub. I turn towards the alcove. No one's there. I rush to inspect the basin. It's empty and dry.

Backing out of the recessed alcove, shaking inside where my stomach curls, I can smell someone else in the house. It's the body odor of a boy dirty after playing outdoors all day. The clash of soap on his sweat-stained skin and the fragrant steam from the hot water meld into a humid musk with an undertone of decay. Unclean hair and clipped fingernails perfume the room like a coffin.

It's normal for an old house to harbor strange smells. Not every maid displays the same dedication my mother once had to her job. I turn to leave.

The Benadryl kicks in hard. The naughty festivity of the wallpaper becomes more sinister. Figures writhe into anatomically impossible positions. Orgasmic mouths gape with pain. Screams of pleasure mutate beyond erotic agony. The aging wrinkled velvet of the vintage paper degrades like a pattern of lichen on a dying tree.

In one moldy corner, inhuman creatures sodomize and soil each other in odd groupings. Figures small and malformed sprout longish ears, curling horns, or prehensile tails. Sown from decades of mildew, genitalia transform into beaks and claws. Nipples grow feral eyes. In the center of a circle of monstrous couplings, a large man mounts a diminutive form. He hovers almost lovingly with huge black outstretched wings.

My broken skin is prickly and hot. My head feels heavy and strange, and I laugh. I always thought my mom restricted my exploration to prevent me from breaking anything of value, to protect her position and paycheck. It looks like there was a bit more substance to her caution than that.

It's true I transgressed into the library once, although strictly speaking, it wasn't my fault. The new assistant, for there was always a new assistant, invited me to help her with cataloguing the Reverend's vast collection. She felt sorry for me, a pathetic kid, isolated by poverty. I played along with her because I thought she was pretty.

Ignorant of my mother's strictures, the assistant explained to me how she cross-referenced the provenance of objects the Reverend acquired from his travels around the globe and recorded her documentation. I pretended to understand, entranced more by the music of her voice than the meaning of her words. Several of the Reverend's antique reference volumes lay open before us. I was old enough to recognize the languages printed on the pages were not English, the illustrations arcane.

I held a grotesque demonic figurine hewn from ebony propped happily on my lap. The assistant steadied my incompetent child's hands with her sure fingers. She didn't see the outrage on my mother's face.

"Lunchtime," my mother said after she caught my eye. It was too early for lunch. She wheeled her mop bucket around the corner. She didn't need to glance back again to make sure I obeyed. I knew I was in trouble.

The Reverend hosted lunch that day at the bright kitchen table as if he had been expecting to dine with me all along. He was rarely home when my mother worked, and had never eaten meals with us. I was excited to see him despite the circumstances.

Tight-lipped and blunt, my mother apologized for my intrusion in the library while the Reverend pecked at a plate of grapes. She slapped a baloney sandwich down in front of me. I toyed with an embroidered linen placemat and peeked up at the Reverend, uncertain what to say.

My mom hovered at the counter with her back turned to me. Reverend Crow spread his arms magnanimously wide, looking from side to side as if the tiny kitchen were a great expanse. The black sleeves of his cloak hung down like elaborate wings. His wire rimmed lenses glinted above a long aquiline nose. I giggled with childish delight at his resemblance to his namesake.

"There's no harm in exposing children to other cultures. Quite the opposite. It's good for them, Lynn. You know I've never held with your coddling."

My mother stood clutching her hands together and failed to meet his eyes. She didn't use my name, as if I wouldn't know who she was talking about. I felt oddly invisible. "This is a sensitive child. We've almost outgrown the nightmares. I told you I can't deal with that again. I just can't."

"Dreams are nothing to fear, Lynn. Isn't that right, little man?"

In the same kitchen where I once made Reverend Crow laugh by slipping a piece of baloney from its mustardy-sleeve of bread, folding it, and taking bites to create a series of small circles signifying a smiley face while my mother fidgeted and stuttered in anger, I now grab ice cubes from the freezer and melt them on my feverish nape to calm the persistent inflammation. Cold water soaks my collar. A trickle sneaks down the small of my back.

The mysterious scratches have progressed from itching to soreness. I search with my phone, worried I've come into contact with some poisonous weed invading the cultivated perfection of Reverend Crow's garden.

No online pictures I find match my wounds. The edges of my scabs bulk with knitted flesh. Raised slits are surrounded by deepening wrinkles that spread from a central spine. The ridges of each scab rise from broken skin, erupting like mountain ranges on a tiny relief map. A reddish-purple feathering that tints the black grooves suggests infection.

Without health insurance or immediate access to transportation, I hunt for volumes on botany in the library, a folk cure to keep me at my post. To be honest, though, it's not the practical concerns that hold me here. I owe a debt of loyalty to Reverend Crow.

The unique grandeur of his house suggested adult life could hold wonders instead of complaints. This is the place where I first glimpsed there might be more than ruined marriages and short paychecks plaguing me into old age. Reverend Crow's example inspired me to leave my family and set out on the road seeking a better life. It's not his fault my travels didn't land me in the mythical palaces of fairy tales, but in alleys and slums.

Yet his house is not the palace I thought I remembered. My imagination built his diminutive library into the forbidden temple my mother feared.

I enter expecting bookshelves tall enough to require ladders, volumes lining every wall, a spiral staircase towering towards a grand skylight. While the shelves hold a smattering of oddities, the vast bestiary of demonic statues I recall is missing. Gone are the taxidermy gargoyles that once flocked upon the mantle, wings arched in protective and predatory stance. Though I remember the warmth from the fireplace and the delicious odor of woody smoke as I nestled beside the assistant's lap, here there is no fireplace, no mantle, no staircase, no skylight.

The library I now find is a stuffy office bordered by a ceiling of normal height. Books stacked in clumsy piles block access to over-burdened shelves. The single stuffed bird is a maize and grey-toned wryneck, its one remaining glass eye etched milky and dull with age.

My false memories balk at the artless clutter. This room is the foundation of my most secret desires, a room that never existed. Careless, I fling volumes down from the shelves.

Sunlight streams through the burglar bars. Botany books scrape my scarred arms. I spread my haul on the floor, scanning tables of contents and indexes for *noxious*, *rash*, and *poisonous*. Yesterday's giddy visuals from my jaunt over the grounds don't conform to the delicate botanical drawings.

The ache and prickling within my skin distracts. My mind wanders. My flesh is striped grey and gold with sunlight and shadow. Bruised wounds align with the brushstrokes of the burglar bars. I wonder if we are born tattooed with the cages we manifest in our lives. As the shadow contrast deepens to black, the yellow blast of a modern photograph revives my dulled power of attention.

I recognize the leaf pattern in the illustration, the shimmering fall gold, and the conical spike of berries. Poison sumac or velvet sumac: one safe, one toxic. They are distinguished only by the color of the fruit.

My skin reacts as if the iron burglar bars seared my flesh through visual contact. Charred shadows darken the hair on my arms. Strands fester in each wound, sooty and black. The central ridges of the slits smooth into slender spines.

I scramble to my feet, fumbling out of this shadow cage of dark and light. My elbow bats an idol crammed onto a shelf. I catch it midair before it breaks. The onyx carving is cool to the touch, sumptuously winged, and as hard as a raven's beak. My unsteady hand slips along the inviting surface of the polished stone. I stroke the elegant sheen of its ornate regalia and place it back on its shelf.

I rush past the mirror in the foyer despite the impression of a blonde boy's head turning to spy my flight. The image repeats, for like all mirrors in this house, it is hung opposite another mirror. My hair has turned dark in the intervening years, I'm glad to say. I do not wish to see who remains trapped in these secret rooms filled with luxury and promise. I don't want to know why new assistants came and vanished with the speed of a magician's trick, why I never met a gardener tending the extensive manicured grounds, or how my mother lasted so long and passed away so soon after leaving Reverend Crow's employment. I burst from the house as I burst out of this town once before, seeking not answers, but a release from answers. Oblivion.

Freedom stifles in the glare of the sun. I will find this tree of poison. I will demand my body back, if only to murder it. I barrel through the orderly rows of roses, too polite to prick me with their elaborate displays of thorns. The pebbled footpath thickens with brambles as I race away from the crumbling old house. Tall perennials whip my arms, petals dropping, seed-heads rattling, autumn overgrowth crushed underfoot. The stick-fingers of small trees pluck at my hands and eyes as dense vegetation crisscrosses my stumbling path. Colors of fire in the dying leaves mirror my inflamed wounds. Flesh tinted the colors of bruises flakes off like paper and flutters behind me in a billowing black wake.

Progenitor trees loom taller, crowding the burning sun, striping me with innumerable black slashes of shadow. I hop through the puzzle of roots, lighter on my feet, hollower in my bones, ebony feathers erupting from my eroding skin. I pierce cascading undergrowth with nimble talons, ever-eyeing the shiny button of the sun that blinks through the black scratches of knitted trunks. Shredded skin seasons their bark, leaving only the sleek plumage that bursts from my chest.

My child skin has fallen away. The forest opens on an unharvested field. Row upon row of brittle stalks host desiccated ears of corn long past the milk stage. Wisps of silk like the hair of beautiful blonde boys populate the neglected field and dry harvest gatherings.

Unshorn head after unshorn head nods under the noonday glare. Silk flies free as the corpses decompose, upright and impaled.

My hollow bones cool as I alight in the field. A central scarecrow greets me with outstretched arms. The sleeves of his vestments hang down like open wings. I recognize the onyx sheen of his sharp black beak; feel its pointed tip lodged inside me as it continues to twist.

A screech of pain forms my core as the beak forever gores me.

Reverend Crow raises his arms higher, flickering across the clouds. A truck rumbles down the long country highway. A murder of crows rises from Reverend Crow's field of rotted crops and wasted lives. Blonde boys line the furrows. Roots run like veins through my grave. I spread my lips to scream an accusation. The sound blurts out in a truncated squawk.

The approaching truck slows. I flap, shout, and scream for help, rousing our congregation, spiraling in manic flight. We override the sun.

The driver stops to gaze at the black tornado. He lights a cigarette and blows pale smoke out of his window.

We whirl in a warning of storm. As fat drops of rain hit the windshield, the driver tosses his spent filter onto the dirt. He rolls up his window. The engine rattles into motion, muting the cacophony of crows. In the center of the field below, Reverend Crow's vestments billow. The flapping fabric mimics laughter.

ECLIPSE, EMBRACE

The huntsman's axe in miniature cleaves the tough pad on the earth side of the animal's paw. Howling skyward, claw extracted, the animal forgets the small wail of stolen blood. As a magical artifact, the claw's lost consciousness resonates in isolation. Inaudible to the huntsman, the animal, and the blade of the infinitesimal axe, the remains of keratin sheath and mangled vein rotate in discordant harmony as if the sun circled a singing planet or the moon maneuvered a new-found orbit.

First the capillaries extend outward, rooting through stone, finding footholds in the flawed rock of the abandoned quarry. Next the blood groove of the claw thickens, re-fossilizing in concordance with protractile mineral tendons inside the curved structure. Passages narrower than single threads vibrate with a venous amniotic message of growth. Perception and penetration fuse. Flesh and fur encapsulate raw stone.

This wolf will not be weighted down and stitched together by huntsman's tricks. Red-cloaked in the guise of a child, this wolf of stone and claw rises with the buoyancy of shed tears. She fills her grave with weeping. From her saltwater slurry, the animal Sophia stays afloat even as the quarry floods. Swollen generosity deposits her ghost in piled sediment on the graffiti-marked cliffs.

Sad enough to split constants, Sophia feels like she has two heads. It's hard for her to be alone in theory, impossible in practice. Deva's due back from town to rescue her again, but Sophia was born in the quarry, born from a claw. Through unforgiving seasons of loss, through arterial congress, through petty theft from kids who vandalize the abandoned quarry for kicks, it's the place Sophia will never leave.

She's pleased when Deva fucks up. It's the same with every job they get. Deva promises to save Sophia from the wild and comes back from town broke again with ridiculous offerings: potato chips, a handheld marine radio with a blown fuse, a lost cat. This time it's fireworks.

The campsite is far enough from the quarry that they don't worry much about cops. Public land allows two weeks per month residence before it's a criminal offense.

Deva sets up their haul around the fire pit left over from the last class of seniors celebrating graduation. In the deep well of the abandoned quarry, sounds bounce off the severe surface of abused basalt and rise into a company of echoes that puts Sophia on edge. A murmur magnifies into a laugh, a laugh into a newborn's scream, and a scream into a chorus of moon-mouths howling as though a cohort of wolves and lovers sprang into orgiastic life from stone.

Sophia listens for intruders between echoes.

Graffiti disappears as the sun sets. Messages lost in the dark. Unspeaking stones circle the monolithic walls of the manmade cavern. Deva unpacks missiles, tubes, and repeaters, happy doing all the labor. They gather branches for the woodpile and get the fire going. Sophia's darting eyes light up with reflected flames.

They're useless, Sophia thinks with gleeful approval of Deva's misplaced enthusiasm. They're serious about putting on a good show, serious about growing old together, serious about providing for the family they fantasize having with Sophia someday. Deva doesn't realize an apartment isn't much different from a cage in a carnival or a museum diorama that turns life into a display. Deep in the woods is the way to run free, love free, and stay off the taxidermy grid until Sophia decides she wants to end it all and get stuffed.

Young as ever, Sophia, with her high pretty voice and dark

animal eyes watches, Deva by daylight and firelight growing older, rougher, less sinuous but no less sensual. Deva prods the logs into a tripod shape, caretaking shy flames at the base. Forearm striations flex. The lines in their face suck down shadows with the fierce thirst of time. Life in the wild is hard on mortal flesh. Deva's meat grows lean from circumnavigating death.

"Go up on the ridge, love," they tell Sophia. "You'll be able to see better from there. Won't be so loud for you."

"What about Cutter?"

Sophia named the cat after bug spray. Deva worked hard to domesticate him when he followed them through town to the edge of the asphalt and into the brush. Cutter's been missing for who knows how many days while Deva was off losing another job. Without saying anything out loud, they've agreed never to discuss how animals act around Sophia.

"Just go."

Sophia wants to say *I'm sorry*, or *won't the fireworks frighten him off for good*, or *we could get pregnant together but not in the way that you think*, but instead she obediently climbs the gravel rise to the lip of the quarry in diminishing luminescence. Slippery bits of rock don't slow Sophia's nimble pace. Nor does her red-hooded cape, threadbare on its ravaged hems and overly long for her childish height. It whips around her sure-footed steps without a mishap.

At the crest where Sophia exits the steep quarry, five boulders are perched, sentries over the gulf of denuded earth marking a gateway between worlds and lives. The open pit gapes empty with decades of disappeared rock. Beasts abused of stone and claw dash down to start anew. Mortals flee for fear of falling. Hawks lift up and away, carrying the sun over the horizon nightly to sink under the earth in slumber. Sophia's unique in holding a mutable and mutated form on the borderline.

The huntsman and his axe live within Sophia still, though surely he's forgotten her face and the sound of her cries for mercy. Murdering wolves is his habit and his calling, and he must be called. *So much time has passed*, she thinks. The spaces between echoes can't possibly hold his footsteps. She climbs on top of the highest boulder to watch the show.

Small and powerless below, Deva bends, a huddled creature scampering to craft flame from sparks. Sophia perceives movement more than identity, will more than art. Untouched by light pollution, the quarry's darkness inks over the edges of Deva's fledgling fire and paints kohl onto the axe blade, forever red emboldened with Sophia's blood.

Here in the place where she was murdered, Sophia feels most at home. The past threat of her disgorging veins is ever-present. A thriving hunger ignites within the strata of inert rock where she intersects with the huntsman's path. Aroused by her touch, the quarry acquired a taste for sacrifice. Exploited geology throbs with loss and a need to live. Sophia feels the cold desire of stone through her cloak, cross-legged atop a boulder.

Hissing, a firebomb shoots upward and vanishes with a whistle. Seconds later, repeated detonations clamor over the basalt expanse. The quarry shudders loud at percussive sounds, reminiscent of its broken past. Lights flash and sizzle near Sophia's eye level. Expectant rock beneath Deva's feet trembles at the next launch. Multicolored lights bloom from the arms of smaller and smaller pinwheels of light exploding in the sky.

Like starfish being born, Sophia thinks. She has the inexperienced and vague misconception that everything in the sea sparkles.

"You wouldn't like it there, no matter how many stars." The huntsman's shadow speaks from behind Sophia in a tone as dense as clay. "You'd sink like a stone. The ocean's made of a million people's tears."

Because he's a shadow, he's invisible in the dark. Sophia's thighs chill through the worn threads of her red cloak. The boulder underneath her freezes in anticipation. The huntsman tests his axe.

Deva hollers up joyous and unaware between blasts. The shotgun sounds of festivity have roused the huntsman's curious aggression with real or imagined war.

He leans over Sophia's shoulder, pulling back the lip of her red cowl. "Let me kill the animal and save you from all this." He whispers. "I'm an expert. No one will be able to tell the difference."

No doesn't sum up every reason his war isn't hers, how the animal is inseparable from the sacred meaning of pursuit, or how the fur and tooth of one girl can swallow as many men as it takes to conquer and close a threshold. Silent, though his axe may strike and miniature in its surgical penetration of Sophia's anatomical vice, the secret damage inflicted on her hits home hard. As it was in the past, the endless forever moment of trauma cracks Sophia in half.

Lights, colors, and shooting arcs— a claw within a claw. Sophia hurls her halves apart. Stone meets axe. Wolf meets man. Sun meets coma. The smell of struck matchsticks writ large and drifting across the quarry undermines the explosive magic of soaring, sparkling lights.

Deva sets off the last and biggest blast with a warning yelp. A cannon sound precedes the finale. Like a vivisected starfish, arms depart the central disk in the sky as stones fall like innards into the huntsman's hands from Sophia's ripped-out stitches. The hot smell of sliding gravel weighs down lingering smoke.

Noises lapse into echo. Memory of sound makes a dying sound.

Hewn by the huntsman's shadow, her heart home to the spirit of his axe, Sophia stops struggling against the forearm crushing her throat and enters the final stages of becoming a statue. The pain from behind guts her like a forsaken clock. She cycles through memories of the future. Above the celestial roof of the quarry she sees into a world that is always spinning, a world where Sophia is always murdered, a world where one single capillary thread must be stronger than stone to survive.

Pressed under layers of sediment, Sophia feels the flow of ground water replacing her soft tissue with minerals. The process fossilizes her vulnerable remains and hardens the tiny spaces between her bones. Her image crystallizes in rock. She ceases to age.

Fixed in time, Sophia's terror casts a shadow with seven heads: a three-headed wolf bites a two-headed man wielding a double-bladed axe. The blade is shaped like children clad in fairy tale cloaks facing opposite directions. Sophia has two heads.

Tangled, the miscreation swirls. Shadow sucks Sophia, inert monument atop her frozen boulder. The quiet sky smells of burnt dynamite. The planet crushes her bones.

Sky clashing in a vacuum that hoards unnatural resources, Sophia teases out a thread thin as a capillary, red as a scream.

Earthward, the yowl of an angry cat contrasts with the aftershock of Deva's show of cacophonous blasts. Through lingering bells that ring an atonal alarm, their injured eardrums catch Cutter's rising hiss and warning howl.

Deva rushes to climb the gravel hillside. Slipping and clamoring up the tricky incline, they scold with nervous agony: "Hey, you up there, behave."

Then they cry out to Sophia: "Are you all right?"

They scramble on the loose surface. No answer but tortured feline shrieks.

Questions shunned by love, doubts too destructive to name, the sentinel gates open on the girl Deva met in the middle of nowhere who says she's much older than she looks. Here atop the liminal crest of the used and ruined landscape, Deva's beloved Sophia stands naked on a boulder with arms stretched skyward. Blood from her nipples drips down like tears, pooling in the cup of her belly button and branching in unraveled threads to take root in the shadow encasing her legs, a fleshy red shadow of renaissance draping, an unraveling.

Deva's flashlight strikes and shoves it back. Folds of glutted shadow ripple down.

Cutter attacks the discarded cloak soaked in darkness below Sophia's boulder. The cat hisses and spits, his ears flat. He circles the edge. With a pounce, Cutter bites the garment and tangles his claws as he kicks. Flipping upright and growling backwards, Cutter drags Sophia's cloak into Deva's beam.

"Easy." Deva hunkers low to Cutter's level. "Let it go now."

Cutter releases his prey and rubs his nose on Deva's knees, claws retracted, a rumble of soft pleasure building in his throat. Threads straggle like uprooted weeds from Sophia's frayed garment. Deva shakes off the surface dirt and climbs Sophia's dais.

Sophia the statue refuses to make eye contact or respond. Deva seeks the source of her bleeding, but the flow has dried and begun flaking off in brownish specks.

Deva wedges the flashlight in their belt and reaches up with care to grasp Sophia's raised hands. One at a time, they bring them down to rest by her sides and tuck her forearms through the sleeves of the cloak. Nestling fabric around Sophia's tensed shoulders and sliding her hair out of the back of the collar, Deva closes the mantle over Sophia's frozen chest. They button up the front clasps and tie the drawstring in a loose bow at the base of her neck.

Cutter leaps up to circle the couple's legs and settles between their feet. Embracing Sophia under the moon, flashlight illuminating a random slab of silenced rock, Deva pulls rigid arms around their waist and leans in against Sophia's stiff hips. Tallest of the two, their gentle grip instructs Sophia's cheek to rest against their chest.

This close, it's hard to tell one body from another. Deva bows their head and breathes in the dirty fragrance of Sophia's black hair tainted with firecracker smoke. Sophia's sediment eases with a suggestion of warmth. Rhythmic movement atop a rotating planet that desperately wants to be made up of more than visible matter encourages Sophia to take a few unconvincing breaths. Deva clutches her in a ghost-hold.

Coma releases. The wolf stitches an origin story from stone. Once again, the bleeding claw, disembodied, moves on a restless axis. Proteins reorganize like faith. Perception and penetration fuse. Flesh and fur encapsulate raw hope.

Deva sings to Sophia as the imperceptible becomes manifest in an early morning eclipse. Sophia weeps a quarry full of tears before she whispers her part in response. Even then, her voice is small, precious, and inhuman. Careless, unbowed before the sun's dark mask, Deva grasps Sophia's body with rough love and doesn't notice the flashlight battery burn out.

I TIED YOUR HEART ON A STRING

I tied your heart on a string. Even though you're fragile and old, the myocardium density of the muscle sheath held firm at the center of mass. I hung it on a hawthorn branch above a three-dimensional cube I sketched in black chalk. No one noticed your heart as they passed by on the sidewalk. No one stopped to see the sketch of the cube smeared beneath their shoes. No one looked up or down. They took the pumping for their own pulse, your drops of blood for rain.

I checked on you three times a day, moving between the tree and the shed where I kept you, fraught with fear of your instantaneous dislocation. I'd come to rely on you. You had invaded my thoughts by proximity and you kept leeching time from my everyday life. You spoke to me in that code you use, the one I'm not sure I will ever get right no matter how hard I listen for a connection. I tried. I am still trying. I will try, again and again.

I'm tired, but I promise I'll try— I'll remain vigilant in pushing back against time. I won't ever sleep again. You mean more to me than temporal rest.

When I check on you, I try to follow the alien thought patterns, the trials and turns of your moods. I know this doesn't make sense. There's something I see in you. A spark of understanding, a twist I can give by accommodating the disorienting rapidity of your action.

I'm trying to explain how confusing all of this is for me moving from past into present and back again. I'm trying to meet you at zero.

In my last check, if you'll pardon the adherence to chronology, your mass seemed to increase or decrease in my absence. For a long period of time you stopped responding. In a frantic attempt to bring you back to what I understood as life, I recounted to you step-by-step how we met and came to inhabit this dark starless moment that feels so endless together on this night in the shed. Reciting unfamiliar facts, I faltered. I wasn't sure if I'd captured you or if you held me hostage in your service. I made up what I didn't know in a frenzied bid to keep going. I'm sure I sounded desperate and unbalanced, but I didn't care anymore. By then I'd lost all shame.

I hoped— I hope we are in love. I still don't know if that's the best way to describe the unstable equilibrium point of our bonding and if we are bonded or not. Your code is too oblique for me. I can know only my own part in this, my choices, and my systematic maintenance prolonging your repeated reversals of time. To avoid your inevitable decline, I check on you three times a day, five times a day, seven times a day, day and night, back and forth between you and the plumb line that suspends your beating heart.

This conflict between two spaces that exclude me, one after the other interchangeably (shed and tree, front and back, in and out) proves your extradimensional freedom compared to my simplicity, your sufficiency compared to my need. I'm running on the fragile hope of a homotopic return, tripping on the lack between going backward and forward in time. When you dropped into my world and onto the wrong map, I sensed by the strange tingling sensation under my scalp that I had to cut out your heart to keep you alive.

I didn't have to lose my mind. I didn't have to act upon you with care and deliberation. I could have let you fade and die.

I cut out your heart because it was too beautiful to bear alone. I saw how it hurt you to hold such beauty in your semitransparent gelatinous chest. I cut out your heart because I was greedy and I wanted to keep your beauty alive in my life, my ugly, loveless life. Like some poet discriminating against science, I refused to accept that all beauty must die, and I built a puzzle to restrain you from topological mutation. I held you. I hold you. I didn't let you phase back to your invariant homeland, transforming within yourself and vanishing from perception in the same sudden peripheral flash as you appeared.

I tied a string through your heart and hung it on a hawthorn branch to hold you here and hide beauty in plain sight. The string doesn't wind across the yard and over the roof and through the alley to the shelf in the shed where you watch me and spin in your jar. The string is too short. I don't have any more to give. Even now, as you rotate slowly behind the glass, I'm not sure I understand the signals or make the connections. Your undulations and jerky movements could mean anything or nothing. They might not even be for me.

The heart is mine, though. It must be. It thrives in the sun where I strung it up, bleeding, pulsing, and resisting the flow of entropy that beseeches it to disintegrate into rags.

The string plumbs from the branch, slick and wet with your blood, a liquid semi-opaque, the color of old amber. It holds. When we started, I cut off a piece of the string to place inside your jar because it wasn't long enough to reach through visible space. I'm still relying on the unseen in our future. When we started, I measured the time it took to pull your heart out through your throat after cutting it loose in your chest, the distance between each one of your many vibrating limbs, and the reflection of light on a knife edge held perpendicular to the center of your heart. I counted the myocardium spirals and multiplied by zero. With the final calculation, I made my cut.

You'll understand the math is a paradox and the process is impossible. The best way for us to connect in real time is to pretend none of this ever happened. The center of your heart is a conjecture.

Are you listening? Awake? Let me tell you how we met, how we meet, how we will meet and depart and will meet again. Listen to the form we take in the future.

I placed the piece of string in your jar. Your many limbs nursed like leeches' mouths at the amber liquid that effused from the segment of string. It responded as if sentient by threading the limbs together to form an asymmetrical flower shape composed of shining tubes. The form was somewhat like a sea anemone, an organism functionally immortal. In the skewed center where your throat still moaned open from my invasive fist, a color like flame arose: gold, scarlet, white, and at the base of the erect stamen a transitory cobalt-blue, like a cock ring carved from lapis lazuli, glowing brightly.

I tied your heart on a string and hung it from the hawthorn branch like a pendulum. It beat the air methodically, its size and swing equal to my small fist. My fist fits around it like a glove when I tear it out and pulled it through your throat. Like a small insistent fist, it still beats and it doesn't know when to stop.

This repetitive violence keeps time. Time keeps your heart. Your heart holds me here. Your amber blood runs up the string and seeps into the segment despite severance. From fluid below the threshold of visible space, continuity grows roots through hidden speculative complexes infusing you like prayer. I hold you there.

I rush to check on you again, again. Your jar floods with amber. You undulate slowly. You send out electrical signals and illuminate the liquid, which rattles the glass and shakes the shelf. The shed remains steady, however, anchored by the certainty of its unimaginative suburban construction, and I'm excited by your signals, excited you're responding again. I'm trying to shake you out of your stasis while keeping you safe. I'm trying to hold you in constant stasis by running back and forth faster than the pendulum race can alter your fluctuating mass. I have faith in your ability to maintain these two opposing states at once.

I won't lose control. No matter how starless this night, I blink only to refresh the contradictory stillness of your speed.

You spin ten times slower than the spiraling myocardial layers of the hanging heart muscles that twist and untwist with each developmental pulse of the pounding fist, swinging in the steady rhythm of the pendulum as I run and check again and again. Back and forth, speeding and slowing, defying the demands of my distressed body, I reek of moss and sweat, having gone too long without a shower or bath. My lips crack. I've forgotten to drink or eat. The way time exists in my body, I'm not made for this vigil, but I hold it. I hold you. I return.

You stare at me like a slug, eyeless. You press your overly lipped mouthparts on the jar. You pretend you have teeth or extra holes where the roots of teeth have dug in deep and bored down into the gums to leave empty channels of holes. Holes amass like inverted limbs, vibrating through the pocked surface of your more loose and spongy parts. I used to worry that you hated me, but now when I look in your cratered mouth, I have no more doubt.

Please tell me you love me. I'm running as fast as I can. I'm trying to meet you at zero. I'm trying to exert a restorative pressure equal to the violence of your displacement and hold you close. I need to hold you without risking your extinction. I need to feel you on my skin, your pockmarked holes like many lipless mouths pulling on the elastic surface of what is seen. I am begging you for this connection in our shared tangible space.

I need to enter your code like the liquid signal that electrifies your amber blood. I hung your heart on a hawthorn branch above a cube sketched in black chalk. The cube fades as excess amber falls, a simple trap eroded, not the best but the best my finite mind could make.

I need to stop us moving forward or backward in time. I swing back and forth, a pendulum trying to keep the center of your heart stable and sharpened to a single point. You exist in too many places at once. Pinning you down to a stable point excludes time. Whetting the knife tip on this map is how we conquer death. I can see it like a graph but I can't explain how this works, how confusing all of this is for me, this moving from past into present and back again so rapidly.

I swing between your points to bring them to zero. I am begging for a sign.

I can't explain the language of your lights blinking in and out like floaters caught in the corner of my eye, invading my thoughts by proximity while stubbornly maintaining a steady distance. Blinking rhythmically like the pendulum swing, like the pummeling fist that closes around a swelling, twisting, screaming heart until its electrical impulses flatline in a rush of panicked discharge and its very eyes and lights go black. What were we thinking when we invented the stars?

The glass rattles on the shelf. I realize I've slept.

The shed is dark but for a sickly glow seeping from your jar.

Your amber blood is suffused with a greenish tinge. An odor of sea rot pervades. The lid is off the jar. What rotates slowly inside appears at first glance like a pair of mating starfish burnt in the midst of their reproductive act and fused in charred ecstasy. As the object turns, the dense liquid reveals a shrunken head with wild black locks. A human face ravaged with sleeplessness and speed, with unwashed hair, cracked lips, and hunger-fraught eyes. Not burned by fire but seared and darkened with time. Not lifeless, though, for its mouth moves in sluggish ardor as if it would speak.

Bubbles percolate from the splintered lips. I try to read the light patterns in the liquid signal, but the code is in some unfamiliar past tense— inadequate to grasp my multiple locations of being forward in time. Simplistic in its funny rhythmic patter, the head drifts in a tight circle, propelled by its bubbling rant as it slides nowhere inside a collapsing dimension.

I recognize the little monkey face, the monkey that swings back and forth between my multiple states. Incremental changes accelerate with each forward pendulum motion reversed. Coming through the cube on the sidewalk sketched in black chalk, employing the functional framework in place, I root in a paradoxical shift, breaking the rotation at our phase point, breaking the axis of a terminal planet.

I hop on the monkey's head. I give it what it wants.

The sensation starts in the scalp, below the skin, close to the skull where a thin layer of fatty tissue quivers. Hair follicles sharpen to pinpoints. Tingling starts. An esoteric sense of omen approaches spasm. Blood vessels grown near the intersection of unrelated planes divide our shared millisecond at cancerous angles. They branch in immediate contact, assimilating time to render it inept. Scalp, skull, and head speed off like past, present, and future suctioned into the ululation of the vacuum yawning between my sewn appendages. I am not a flower. Popping loose, un-mouthing prehensile tubes leak unlimited anemone holes as the swallower of light regurgitates light. The smell of exchange is simultaneous: a fire's gasp.

The indigestible lump of the monkey's head is excreted into amber. I'm pleased by the cylindrical match of its anatomical errata, with the way my asymmetrical form finds circular footing atop its meaty neck, and with the robust beat of the replacement heart. An old heart shreds in a tree outside as twisted rags disintegrate. Monkeys hang such rags as prayer. I stand, elevating my new vehicle, curious to experiment with the hybrid apparatus fixed in finite space.

Atonal humming vibrates from the open jar. Darkness reigns, my gift. This planet's over-exuberant sun doused, the air is as dark as the bottom of its ocean, and the glow of old blood from the jar emits a jaundiced radiance within the shed. Green bubbles seep through ruptured lips like slow rot. Cracked lips pucker, stretch, and mewl. The little monkey head suspended in amber chatters as if it would speak to me:

"I tied your heart on a string. I hung it on a hawthorn branch to hold you here. I hid your beauty in plain sight. I cut out your heart because it was too beautiful to bear. It hurt you to hold such beauty in your chest. I was greedy. I wanted this beauty to stay alive in my life, my ugly, loveless life. I don't know how to explain. I need to hold you and feel you against my skin. I'm trying to explain how confusing all of this is for me, moving from past into present and back again. I'm trying to meet you at zero. Please tell me that you love me. Tell me this is love."

BELOVED OF FLIES

They cut him in half and filled his body with flies. He had no pain although he was conscious the whole time. Some method of hypnotic anesthesia must have been employed to mimic a dream and force him to comply. Attaching his severed halves, their seamless suturing knit his body cavities closed and whole as he lay stunned in the black hum. By the end of it, he appeared unchanged to the naked eye despite the horde of flies sealed inside.

He felt at once astir with their restless twitching antennae, legs, and whatever one called a fly's searching tongue. *Proboscis maybe,* he thought. His thoracic cavity whirred with the busy gyrations of interrupted flight. Trapped wings in constant motion thwarted the flow of oxygen to his lungs. Once his panic subsided and he realized he was not drowning, he began to enjoy the new sensation crawling through each teeming breath. Found the shaky, throttling work of it a comforting task.

Colonized, he felt strangely safe. No longer one, he was many.

He tried to explain what had happened, but his mother didn't understand. His voice came out hoarse, changed by the fitful resonance of the captive horde. They reproduced and roiled in his diaphragm. His pelvic cavity squirmed with new larvae.

She told him to do his chores. She repeated herself when he

couldn't hear over the humming from his chest and throat. Flies whirred in his sinuses and behind his eyes. They made a crackling sound in his hollow ear canals.

He wondered if they would burst through every pore in an effort to escape. The pressure within him grew as they bred. Hidden movements made him dizzy and sick; less an impairment to him and more a pleasant reminder he was no longer alone but occupied and something bigger than a simple, single boy.

"I need you to clean your room before dinner. This has gone on long enough." His mother enunciated louder than normal, head half-turned over her shoulder. In the corner, she swept up black specks from a crevice where the baseboards didn't square.

He opened his mouth to argue and snapped it shut when he realized he'd release more flies. He didn't want to make her job harder. She already seemed annoyed.

My room, he repeated, testing the idea. It felt false, a contradiction to his new experience as a collective entity. Sluggish with the burden of moving a multitude, he also puzzled over the concept of "clean." Flies ever-writhing flitted through his cranial cavity, sticking and tingling beneath the hard shell of his skull. Black specks of thought flashed by unidentified. The names of objects seemed meaningless and interchangeable: shirt, hockey stick, headphones.

Dead things were in the room. If some tissues inside him rotted from the damage of feeding maggots, that same rot soon bloomed fecund with abundant life. Unlike the inanimate tokens scattered around him, he became. He multiplied as the flies mated, laid eggs, hatched, fed, molted, pupated, and matured. His body grew hungry.

Hungry with the fullness of a god who ravenously tethers souls both past and present to bring together the squirming and explosive evolution of those belonging in his fold, stars strung deep into the history of an impenetrable galaxy. Stars glinted omniscient at the black edges of his corrupted vision. Generations begged for fulfillment.

His stomach was full and alive. As he pawed the wall away from his room and crept down the hallway, his gut overflowed. Hard brown egg sacs and soft white pupae dribbled from between his lips. A black swarm rose above his back.

"What on earth are you doing?" his mother said.

She had seen him stumble naked into the kitchen, smash open a ceramic canister, and dive onto the floor to lap up spilled granules of sugar, bloodying his tongue on the broken shards.

She said, "Put your clothes on." Calmly, with a mother's practice, as if it were a normal thing to say in a normal situation; but her eyes locked on him, wide. She backed across the room as he arose, her tall naked son, peppered with sugar and blood, surrounded by a revolving halo of flies.

His ears abuzz with breeding, he tried to pantomime the black exam capsule where they cut him in half. The scar that would confer evidence of his bisection elusively teased away from his fingertips: the faint line between his eyebrows, the gentle dent in the cartilage in the tip off his nose. He traced the bony dip at the base of his throat, the hard strip of his sternum, the symmetrical path down the knot of his belly button, and the tiny seam at the tip of his glans.

The scar hovered invisible above his skin and suddenly he realized he had no way to know if the other half they'd attached was the same one he'd started with.

If this other half were not his original half, where was he? Did he think for both with a bisected brain? Was he in two places at once, or alive in one and dead in the other?

His thoughts were here and then gone, flicking between blackness and omniscience. In the instant he saw he was nowhere, the hunger that moved him exploded into an engulfing black swarm shaped like a tidal wave. He leapt at the trembling woman across the room with his teeth and clawed fingers bared.

They caught him in midair. They cut him in half again. Crudely, for they hadn't prepared for this. He endured death with every life pried from his flesh as they extracted the embedded generations of eggs, larvae, pupae, and flies. They cut away the beloved until he was only a fragment of mind.

From his hands and knees, he looked up when it was done. He wanted to cry out but he couldn't vocalize with his newly-repaired tongue. His mother hooked her elbow under his arm and put her full strength into lifting him. She maneuvered him through spilled sugar and ceramic shards back to bed. His brain replaced by scar tissue, he had no choice but to rest.

She pulled up a blanket to cover him and brushed bloody sugar granules off his chin with her thumb. "You're not yourself since the accident. The room can wait."

The silence ached. He longed for the restless chorus of the horde piling onto a fresh feeding site, the hungry maggots moving their mouths, fondling him in a frenzy of eager delight. Exalting in their thousand joyous gulps of connective tissue, of epithelial lining and nerve; weakening with their heightened ecstasy as they ingested strong filaments of his willing muscle and singing as one with the voices of a thousand shiny wings seeking flight.

Empty of all memory of those who fed upon the god, for they had only existed in the cracked temples of his wounds, on his side, silence so loud, his ear against the pillow. Inside the pillow, a crackling sound. Through the hollows in his ear canal, it transmitted a consistent and rhythmic buzz. A murmur not of downy feathers or shifting bedsheets but of insect wings.

He, beloved of flies, pressed his ear to the pillow, willing survivors to find passage and lay eggs. A fertile breeding ground driven by the torrent of a million devouring lives.

His mother's thumb lay on his chin less than half an inch from his mouth. Her face flushed when he started sucking. He pulled her deep inside his mouth and closed his eyes. She didn't resist as he slobbered in silent gratitude that she finally acknowledged what she had surely understood within the black hum yet pretended to fear all along. Then he bit down and kept biting until they were many and one.

FIVE VISITATIONS

The first visitation begins on the surface of her skin, the sensation of bath water warmed to prickle upon immersion. As it escalates from the strange recovery comfort of pins and needles in a numb limb into something both hotter and sharper, or perhaps colder and sharper; yes, that's it, more like ice as if her cells have been frozen and the shards within them slash the walls in a sudden thaw, she collapses, unable to see or speak or scream.

Forming prophecy out of trauma, the world decides to keep her alive. There's no god in this world just like there's no narrator in this story. There's only a body subjected to experimentation in a vacuum she'll designate as her own private hell when she gains enough consciousness to think linear thoughts.

For now, she inhabits a circle of unknowing. Picture it as a halo like a migraine spinning fiery insulation to hide our faces from her perception and protect us from human infection. Hell is never private, and Heaven less so. Thus, this body in between sequences of the experiment vacates intangible space with the suddenness of great pain, pain intolerable to her infant body. Even when she grows older and learns to speak, she will not learn how to speak of such pain except through acts of violence.

The second visitation erupts from a fever forcing her to

remember the first. The words unleashed when she speaks in tongues convince the adults she's gifted, and because this is not the age of carnival barkers but of tests, we administer her tests as participants hidden within her cells. The body floats up from the exam table. She watches it rise. Sudden ectoplasm spits out in a slimy waterfall as memory's chasm vomits obfuscations: taps under the table, broken candlesticks, recordings that sound like the devil in reverse anthem, reverse pride.

A surgeon's touch is like unto us, like an operating table and a sewing machine mating in Hell. He manipulates the levitating body as it vibrates with pain. She splits, and we experience her multiplicity within our many temporal surgical bodies.

Her motion like a bird between branches teaches space to stay riven in contrast with black blood extracted, analyzed, and returned, leaving no detectable scars. Close inspection invalidates her claims of invasion. The body agonized by silence remains aware it has been hollowed out.

The third visitation comes after all visitations have ceased. She craves them. With a vacuum underneath the superficial disguise of skin, the body seeks pain severe enough to fill it. We realize by now the experiment has gone terribly, horribly wrong but we are both too perversely intrigued and admittedly, regrettably, indulgently, too helpless to try to stop.

She, in her psychic medium garb, submits to the doctor's inspection in a private suite before the séance begins. The patron's mansion allows this extravagant investment in time, security, and veracity. While the suite is equipped with vital creature comforts, basic medical instrumentation, and modern plumbing, the doctor's preferred devices of purity assessment hide within the black case by his side until the outer door is locked.

Shroud of divination lifted for his viewing, she turns and bends as instructed. The body on display knows the doctor's evaluation procedures. Séances for weekly society events require his attendance. Not that he objects. Neither does she. Her pleasure escalates into insatiable hunger over the course of months as he examines more thoroughly, more elaborately, more creatively to authenticate her gift by exposing hidden recesses of deception. The lady of the house remains sanguine hearing the screams and moans behind the door, heralds of the ecstasy of spirit possession soon to come. She gathers guests within audible distance as both titillation and proof. Soon the doctor emerges to announce there is no hoax.

Not yet, not yet. The body is too much a mystery he enjoys engineering. Training it to take more pressure here, more pain there, her pleasure balanced and tamed by suffering, by tenderness, by medication administered in precise doses, he forces it to conform to his private vision of exploded lust. He enters into the rich space of our silence, both bidden and reviled by the body, knowing she will accept more pain because she has always accepted, has always returned. Yet he cannot explain what he finds there.

The medium glimpses the endgame in his desire before the doctor knows his own will. Sequentially distant, encapsulated by our forgetful shiverings, we explode from the rift of his vivisection. The couple is exhibited like splayed animals, pinned in place, peeled open from the center, positioned front to front, and sewn together so their internal organs slide and press in wet contact. This includes their faces. Optic nerves and brain tissue will grow into one huge orb of acute sentience. The inescapable intimacy of hearts slapping together raw and the slippery muscle, vein, and fat of membranous hidden life will weave into one liquescent flesh. His vision shudders inside her. Fever shakes her bones and lights the bodies on fire. Where she connects to him, molten metal forges our new minds from empty chaos.

When we wake, we dream of death.

Perhaps we've lost more than our objectivity as yes, oh, yes! We dream she kills him. Because the pain is too much, and yet not enough. Because she's used him up. We see it like we have seen Orion's fires. We are infected. We are insane. We are in love.

After her masterful performance at the séance she'll wait in the dark alley by his house. She'll call softly as he goes by. He'll come to her without fear, merely annoyed, what about his wife; and her dainty clasped hands will shoot between his legs with the knife, disabling him by castration. A near miss, too, will provide adequate shock.

She'll leap back as he grabs his groin and then lunge forward aiming for his throat. We must wait for later to live through the joyful details, the risk of public blood, the feast. Here in the mansion suite the tumescent doctor fills us and we can taste his death as our conception cleaves reason and we are she, she is the body, and our prophecy screams.

The fourth visitation comes repeatedly, a lifelong multiple orgasm of murders reverberating out from the first. Yes, they get better as time goes on. Yes, she delights in her hunger, her hell, her thirst. The body cannot be a lone martyr to rape and yet it also cannot be separate and safe. It, she, and we must hunt.

We, the alien entities masquerading as cells perform our operations in the forgetfulness of the dark. If we, she, I could recall the worst and first pain, perhaps I could purge myself of this need to cut through the meat. I keep a collection of their dried and pressed cocks, for they are my lovers as long as they last. I root for every new one to make it out alive.

Five by five by fire by knives, this is the way another boy dies. They call me Jane the Ripper on the news. I wear no disguise. When I tell him this to his face, he doesn't flinch. He doesn't believe me yet. We have driven our pain past his limit and he is helpless in the restraints. I take my time dividing him.

I walk up to the edge of history and strip naked. I call out over the burning cliffs of an apocalypse and hear no answer but my own voice. I swallow the dark black blood of his pain into the girl-shaped space below my skin. It yawns for succor, ever-empty and bleeding with invisible light. I am many things in one wound. Parts of him I sever to plug and perforate what asks in me to be broken. A fist, an arm, a femur— more is never enough.

The fifth and final visitation is the infection made flesh. I can't do the readings anymore. Tiny dots of light dance in the corners of my eyes. Ambivalent voices slurred by age and drunkenness offer our unemotional apology that the experiment has gone terribly, horribly wrong. We admit we've let it go on for far too long. Spinning the hot halo of abandoned deceit we surround her like dancers on the head of a pin and invite the diseased body to reunite with its original pain.

Her deathbed is a door. The body needs infancy as a narrator. In the same way, our populous mouth of Hell needs actualized prophecies or gods to pin on an operating table. We whisper into the vacuum. Our words crack with pain. She splits and splits again. Mad with the memory of hunger, we swallow our cells like icicles or broken glass. We call into the broken places where we cannot see or speak or scream. We are begging, pleading. Come into the light.

PIGMAN, PIGMAN

Green muddy grass holds boot-prints in the struggle; boy thrashing, screen slips and falls, flash of knife and open mouth as camera eye wrestles with impossible perspective. Your friends run, laughing. Rancid smell of old leather; you can't believe the mask wasn't cleaned better considering the cost, but like everyone else you've agreed to play your part.

Flannels and flashes of elbow, guttural sounds ejecting human loss, camera phone muffled. The eye in your pocket sees better than you behind the Pigman's mask.

Background noise: a girl screams. Grappling men, or man-like things; hungry pig breath of mutual desire grown labyrinthine in soft boy exile. Don't get carried away, though. Unspoken teleology, signals louder than exegetic screams. Start with the boy to keep things spicy.

You allow him the hunting knife. Sensory let-down after the overload of attack. Unshuttered eyes leap through multiple frames. Below the boy's assaulted breast, grunt and shove, wrestle ineffable hands through the car window. Blade work inept against heavy yellow workman's gloves, distressed boy-breath escalates. Gloves drag him out of the car. This can't be happening. Wait a minute. Stop.

He says stop. The gloves fit his neck. Your yellow hands huge and his head a balloon atop the clenching heft— he'll do anything you say. Them's serious words for a boy with no pants.

The camera's getting the performance of their lives from your friends. Are they, though? Who can tell who your real friends are the way they joke but no one's joking now. Boy pleads, girl screams, Pigman grunts.

Outside of the shaky eye, shaking to hide amateur actors and inept effects. But if you do say so yourself, this shot is looking pretty damn legit.

Boy's tongue like a lizard pops out. Will it grow back if you bite it off?

It's all in fun. Blood spatter and strangled silence. You've seen this before in other movies and this Halloween night you're claiming the predator's mask. No grief for teenage meat less tender than your eternal hurt feelings. Deadened by off-screen screams, the assailant fills the frame, panoramic in your plaid, your coveralls, your fleshy rented mask.

Pig breath fogs the lens. Playing the villain like the hero you are. Boy disposed, a hilarious corpse. Cut to the source of the off-screen screaming.

No title card. No credits. No knowing gag to alleviate tension. You want them confused, upset, questioning reality, feeling what it feels like to live inside the madman's mask. The ultimate director's cut is a blade held by heavy yellow workman's gloves.

Camera eye thrusts into Pigman's gullet. Strange carapace frames the soft pink palate. He tests it with his teeth. Pig gloves swing, eye of lens on pelvis as he waggles. You hear him better in his hand.

Snuffling down the road where the girl's stopped screaming. She could flag down a car but she's standing there stupid, tits hanging out. Lifts an arm and aims it at you.

Pigman, Pigman, mind your listing, tilting approach. She's watching like a witch at a square dance. Swing your partner. Swing your axe. The weight of narrative momentum slows the camera to sludge.

When Pigman's stomach growls, you hear his hunger. Grunting

and heartbeats: listen for him in your inner ear on opening night, paraded above the popcorn crunch.

Come on, girl. Let's see you run. It's either slasher or farce. Chase the disheveled girl until bad focus overtakes her sweaty face and promises a rape. Your breath inside the mask sends a wet scent recirculating the legend's stench. You smell the skin who wore the skin before you, the head of a butcher inside the head of a pig.

You're ready to rut up the back of her party dress but she doesn't run. She stands and stares. Next to a stop sign up ahead, arm rigid, gaped-mouth like a ghoul, she points at you.

Pigman wheezes soft in your ears. Eyes of divergent camera phones watch at weird angles in settling night. Nothing moves. Girl steady, disheveled, your would-be victim still as a pillar of black salt.

Something ain't right. Not you. You use good grammar.

The hand holding the phone shakes more than before. Or does the cannibal wrist tremble with neurological disease? Eyes through pig slits pinched into thin edges blink too small to see what's happening at the crossroads.

Chopped up images under the blinking stoplight. Colors changing. Girl twists from left to right. Her limbs look incorrect.

You call out, your voice childish inside the mask.

"Hey, you all right?"

She twists strangely, a spider made of black smoke.

Won't answer. Why would she? Inside Pigman apology becomes a lecherous grunt, but you try. "Sorry that scene got so wild."

Moving closer, under the flashing stoplight, something wrong with her face. Darkness crawling, writhing. And something white. Glinting in her jaw, whiteness spreading, slashing across the midnight black.

Arm aimed at you, pointing, bobbing.

Her mouth bursts black, red, yellow, green as reflective teeth reveal her raucous laugh in the stoplight's flash. Wide open laugh, party dress of tatters, girl of smoke points and twists and wails.

Tugging, the rented mask clings. It seems to like your skin. Missed the snug fit of a face since the last Halloween lynching. You wrestle and snort. It clings to your cheeks.

Caged breath fogs inside with damp heat. Your protest surges into squeals.

Fight, Piggy, fight. Camera jumps and slashes. You plead, confined: Stop. Help. Your plaintive voice, muffled beyond human disguise, heaving outward in frantic breath, reborn as a barnyard bray.

Pig panic rising, short tail curled to your butt, haunches shrinking, lard loading into your teenage gut. Coveralls fall from sloped animal shoulders. Camera drops under knocking hooves. Hairy pink teats fill the frame. Hooves from wrists pummel pink flesh. Pigman tears at his own face.

The sliced off nose exposes your snout. Lights, laughter, flashing: cars are coming, police are coming, everyone's laughing.

Horrific squeals of impotent misery, hooves hurling barnyard heft towards the cover of cannibal woods, phone eye trampled. The footage stops on blood-grimed teats smeared by the crunch of a murdered screen.

STUDIES AFTER THE HUMAN FIGURE

In the first dream, Julia and I are in the studio. I've come back with supplies and a superficial wound, no more than a scratch. She pushes my face away when I try to kiss her. I slink off to pout, but she snatches me back and shows me where she wants it. My face between her legs.

She's naked, even though when the dream starts, she's wearing a white tank top and jeans. The drape sheet we use for life-modeling slips off her shoulders. Fast forward: she's on the floor undulating like I've been lapping at her for a long time. She lunges into me and swallows my chin. My neck's in her labia, nose in her muff. Top teeth and tongue trap her pleasure button and ring it. I drive three fingers inside to push her over the edge.

Julia spreads on the white drape sheet like a transparent starfish constructed of light. I know her from a million different angles. I see every perspective unfold. She's wet around my fingers, so wet I want to slide inside her from behind. I finger-fuck her smaller hole and she responds with high-pitched sighs.

I'm hard and cold and feverish. The wound (nothing but a scratch) weeps through the bandage. Julia clutches my tongue inside. She's stolen my speech and all I can do is grunt and go deeper to get it back.

Then everything changes. Her taste goes from cream to metal. Something fecal and full of iron undermines Julia's sweet scent. In my mouth, she's not smooth as a pearl. Instead she's crammed with something crumbling and jagged and hot. Maybe I bit too hard, maybe she started today. I'm not sure what's happening, but Julia's on fire and I can't stop. I furrow deeper as she struggles and screams. I push forward and get on top. I mount a wet, shifting place, and I'm inside of her with one blind thrust.

Face-to-face, licking and panting at her neck, Julia's light skin is slathered dark with blood from below. She kisses me (doesn't she?) and we're stuck together in every possible way, turning each other inside out. I come and collapse. Julia goes cold.

She stares up at me, a porcelain doll with enameled eyes. The translucent skin below her lower lids cracks with blue veins that spread and turn black. Icy damp clings to my cock. I pull it out. The flood of her entrails slops onto the drape sheet in a dense cluster, a stinking morass.

Julia doesn't move. The cavity fucked open in her abdomen gives birth to a well of dead organs. Surfaces shine with sticky bile, seeping putrescence, and subdermal fat.

My fever breaks. I've been covered in Julia for days.

The blood on her neck and breasts is a dry, brown powder. Gobbets of salty tears spatter out of my face and disrupt the stale burgundy crust. It flakes off from the moisture of my futile regret, the bloating and shrinking of her flesh, the indifferent deconstruction of death.

In the second dream, Julia is dead at the beginning. She keeps talking to me, though. Not like when she was alive and we ran away to the studio and fell in love. Not like when we lied to my mother about the life-drawing class where we met. And not like when we had nowhere else to go but the studio to hide from the hazmat sweeps when I first got sick. Julia doesn't tell me everything's going to be okay like she used to when she was alive.

We both know it's not.

"Your teachers lied to you. They tried to keep you from seeing me, tried to stunt your gift. You're not a witness. You're not an indifferent camera recording events."

My line work jolts and falters. My shading isn't for shit. I can't manipulate the charcoal with finesse or precision anymore, and the paper's crushed and bent. My fist makes brute swipes like an animal's paw, like some stupid abstract expressionist.

"Come closer," she says. "I'll show you all my secrets. You have my solemn promise. Get in the picture with me."

The apparatus of the sketch book and the Masonite drawing board block my view. My nose itches. I rub it with the back of my knuckle. It swivels like loose gristle. I'm worried I smeared my face with charcoal, worried my nose might fall off, worried about what Julia thinks when she sees me like this.

I can't let her see me like this.

I can leave her. Give the usual justification that we need supplies. It's safe for me to go out since I'm already sick.

But really, I'm looking for a new excuse to avoid biting off her breasts. They stare me down like predatory owls, like twin-pimple geyser skins, balloons poised under a pin that tremble for one illicit twitch to make them pop.

The last pristine portion of her left.

I can't.

"I can't do that. Now hush and stay still. I'm trying to work."

"You think you picked me as your model and muse, but I chose you to come here and study me. Listen to what I'm telling you. How can you even stand it? It's so blatant, so gratuitous, so shameless. Can you see how ruthlessly I'm exploiting you?"

"Me? No way. For what?"

"For the luxury of being seen. You vivisect me with your eyes."

"That doesn't sound good."

"God, yes. It's terrifying."

I drop the charcoal from my useless Neanderthal grip and crawl on my hairy knuckles over to Julia's side. "Then why do it? For money? For kicks?"

"Because the work constantly changes me. It changes you, too. I know you feel it happening. The work is making us into something new. Come closer."

"I am closer. I'm right here."

I nudge her when she doesn't answer.

Animal confusion gluts my grunting face with fear.

Dead eyes don't blink. Julia's pale, purple-veined body shows an unsettling flatness at the hips and thighs. Her most voluptuous sections of flesh conform to the hard plane of the floor. The drape cloth bunches in failed disguise, too ripped and blood-spattered to maintain the ruse of a classical representation of beauty or life.

Julia's beauty is (was) in her intellect, her honesty. She bullies me to reach greater aesthetic heights.

I grovel, nudge. "I'm here, right here."

Grovel, grunt.

"Nonsense, kid. You're miles away. What did Witkin say?"

Her lips don't move. Somehow they emit her voice: charged, relentless, demanding. The teacher who will tear me apart: "What did he say?"

"The mark is the primal gesture."

Satisfied, she lies.

I wait for more. I've hung on her words and moods for months. I don't know how to think without her voice.

Silent, the tools of my trade surround me. They populate my pockets and stain my palms. My mark is on everything: fingerprints in charcoal and blood, lip prints in semen and saliva. Life studies of Julia pinned on the walls. Below them, her exploded abdominal cavity, her perforated mound, her sex that opens like a torn flower, stinking of bitter herbs and dancing with white maggots. Disco rice squirm under the million eyes of a mirrored ball, the million drawings of her eyes.

I curl inside Julia's womb and fail the drunk-test of the dance. I'm too large, too cumbersome, too full of recently-ingested flesh.

No, no, no: she rises in my gullet.

I clasp my hands over my mouth to hold her savory parts inside.

———

In the third dream, I begin to understand I'm not dreaming.

Julia's death has outlasted any reasonable human grief. When I was a man, I wasn't reasonable. I was an artist. I'm something different now, something unreasonable and unmanned. At times, my bowels or eyes or limbs don't work. When I'm blind, I crave her most. Over and over again.

Though I succor within her exposed cavity, I can't be born a new maggot. I'm too big and too brown. I never learned to dance. Her small white parasites writhe on my large dark one, crushed to death against bone or drowned where she liquefies. Sweetness creeps back into her scent, a heavy death-musk like roadkill drenched in a semi of spilled perfume.

The taste of her liqueur arouses more than it feeds me.

Julia's genius resides in her ability to simultaneously embody artifice and pose as an objection to it. Remember Witkin, she said, sitting nude. She touched me, our secret. Remember Leda, she said, holding me after class; the amputations, the visible and invisible omnipresence of rot, the voluptuousness of decay. Take note of this (she fondled me, it was wrong) remember this view, what you see from this angle (she was my first) inside me. Julia's genius is (was) in recognizing the object as observer, the voyeur as blossoming cunt.

Where I taste her rising stench, I cower inside. Her aging meat is wasted on my sterile eye. I devour what isn't fresh and choke my desire on death.

Outside the studio window, real life rages and jumps. A flicker, a flounce. The need that moves me is ready to pounce. Tender, moving flesh escapes my craving teeth, but Julia, my love in stillness, in anamorphosis, my model, my mentor, my last meal: Julia knows the animal we've become is unwilling to get out. Frantic, I rub my turgid parasite against her sternum, and break apart the stillness of her dry, stale breasts.

In the fourth and final dream, I enter the dream of the animal, which means I am wide awake.

I tear and crumple the sketches. I cram them inside her. I make a nest. The mirrored walls of eyes are silenced. Where maggots used to dance, I soak up the sanctified drippings of Julia's intimate apocalypse.

(She was my first and)

Cradled and caked in her clotted scraps, I tug the loose stool between my legs named masterpiece. The flab of its rubber casing puzzles me. It has a spine inside, making it rise. I rub it like a bone begging to be interred, like a lover yearning to subvert love's command. I rub open the fine scars of the cross-hatched casing. My emaciated pate tingles in time with a new crop of dynamite disco rice.

Love is but a rendering of our mortal flaws.

Inside-out, the animal of love kills what it becomes.

(Things that howl break the)

Unstrung wires quiver in my throat to release (her) sounds and fluids. The animal escapes us, leaving less than a shroud. Drape sheet like a brown and burgundy tanned hide holds totem relics. The magic I find in Julia is destroyed by my knowledge of it. Words incanted on the hide disintegrate into hieroglyphs and nonsense, less cogent than the beast-lines of Lascaux. Lucid, I forsake her form and cling to the thin pulse that gorges me.

(cry, can't you)

The magic wand in my palms displays injury from non-stop frottage. All that remains of my (first, only, everlasting) model is a translucent mass staining the shroud-brown drape sheet, a drain-clog of hair and tendons lodged in my throat, and bone cairns that defy my broken teeth with the persistence of (pain) memory.

What was edible, I ate.

Her heart won't beat in me. Her brain won't deduce. Her veins won't thrum, no matter how I plead. Every part of Julia that I've stuffed inside of me (the mark is the primal gesture) refuses to give me the answer to how her beauty is constructed, what space in her holds forth unquenchable light, and who she was and will (not) be.

What I was (not) to her.

Again I force the spine to rise.

Again, again.

Pummeling sends a signal through my disintegrated neural

chains. Frail paths ping with the memory of (addiction) sex. Pain constricts as pressure (stop) builds (please stop) into a scream. Weeping, shrieking, trapped. No transgression saves us. No cure waters my eyes.

Hungry, so hungry, oh God, please (don't) stop.

Ghost sighs exit our dry bones. Torn casing deflates. My skinned cock lies between us, a flayed parasite in deliquescent waste. A single maggot squirms out of the slit at the tip.

Parasites long dead, our hunger eats us alive.

This is how we (end) do it. This is how we (be)come.

ALL THE RAPES IN THE MUSEUM

And then by divine insight I knew you were more than another victim dumped in my cell. Disguised as one more mute shaking in the corner— for many have passed in the years or minutes I have survived this lightless dungeon— at first you refused me. Choosing to shudder nude in the damp hay as if the garb of human warmth I offered was tincture of strange poison, bearing witness to my tests when put to the question and suffering likewise in yours; you through the drama of our trials revealed a slow mystery. Mirrors of tortures borne, we cracked the cold silence of the plane dividing us when you left your suit of corporeal illusion to enter the iron maiden and commune with me.

Heretic, remember when my fingers walked upon your skin like Lilliputian legs, traversing your torso, nape, and spine, exploring every inch of your trembling in the long cold dark between interrogations? You were my promised land. I dwelled in you with my forbidden tongue's intent, with a language of creation burning away the euphemisms that normalize violence, with your figure fingered into hierarchical revenge.

My knifeless Spartan queen between assaults, you gave me respite in the steady pain of your brutal consistency, in the many needles of your open arms. One door to the left; one door to the right; both closed to clasp me in a deadly embrace as if we could cocoon as one. The tips of your needles pressed feathers into my skin from forehead to belly to feet, and body captive on those trembling, sharp, and relentlessly present pinpoints I began to see— to really, truly see— the wings withheld in yours.

Your gift of surprise, magic of compassion; yes, it's true. I was ready to give up. Ready to die. We were broken, chipped, and faded. Our martyred cracks could never be restored. Together beset by many rapes, we both knew the futility of this endless investigation. We knew none escaped these chains once they were swallowed up and sunk deep inside the hidden bowels of this museum where accusation equals guilt.

The institution stripped us. They made us watch. Where there were shadows, they shined a bright light to expose our aesthetic flaws. When in agonized resistance at knife point I turned away from the sight of the seventh soldier drilling his syphilis into your limp and collapsing form, his armor clattering as his gut heaved back and forth, his unwashed buttocks clenching and unclenching, his hateful thrusts breaking what was already broken in you; when I at last turned away in defiance and they pressed the edge of the blade to my throat and my carotid artery thumped against the metal and the metal warmed; when they said watch or we'll kill you, we'll kill you and fuck your dead body, I said *Good*, for I had learned that much of their language.

I looked them in the eyes and I said *Do it*.

No buoyant slash released me. These same foreign pale men who claimed the bravery of godlike judgement and reveled together homogenized in godlike exercise of power proved too small of will to shoulder the due burden of my murder. The silent violence of their secrecy exceeded the blunt violence of their abuse. They would delegate my death.

They locked me inside the iron maiden. This device shaped like a welcoming cocoon embraced me with her ineluctable threat. The right door closed first, and then the left. Both doors closed over my screaming face.

I trembled on the points of many spikes and dared not move lest my vulnerable body suffer countless impalements. The cocoon was tightened at intervals, moving the spikes closer to the surface of my skin each day or hour or minute. I no longer understood time. Weakness from starvation and my terror of slumping in my sleep poised my enfeebled flesh tensely across the tips of the iron needles. The metal pressed. Slow punctures emptied my veins, my bladder, my hissing lungs. The damp cold of the dungeon became raging heat as fever flared in my wounds and my obstinate physical instincts preserved me, rejecting infection from the many stinking holes. You also stank, my dead angel, my fallen one, a slumped corpse left for horrific edification that I might witness an example of my own imminent decay.

More time passed. The cocoon tightened again, again. And behold!

You came.

From your muteness into speech of the body, speech of elixir from flesh and radiant hallucinogenic poisons no longer strange but gilded, illicit, and certainly sacred, you comforted me. Angel or demon undefined, you came *from, through,* and *with* death. You left your shadowed corpse and met me without fear. Perhaps you are not an angel of God but an angel of death. I don't know.

I don't care.

And truly, brashly, unapologetically— though it may be impossible and unwise— I welcome you with my memory clear and fond awareness of my full acceptance anew every time you come to surprise me and share with me yet another death.

I match my form to yours in carnal gestures, my imprisoned fingertips now free to trace the planes of a lucid geometry once concealed in life from the hunger of my touch; but no more, no more. These golden means of rigid anatomy fondle free in death. Here are your wings. This is your crown of many feathers. These are your many unblinking eyes. Wisdom may, from misfortune and with unexpected grace, assume a forbidden and monstrous disguise.

Confined and combined— in the cocoon of the iron maiden for months or days or minutes, we feasted on the raw energy of our newborn masticating flesh. We grinded our starved palates against a liminal and vast want; sipped the cup of our sex-gushed sweat, saliva, and tears. We grew obscenely drunk on the excess of our

liquid macerations. We thrived without need of any natural susten-
ance outside the scorched fumes of our nutritious dying bodies.

I saw the truth of you in your sudden and unexpected compre-
hension of lust, a lust essential in our rebellion against torture.
When we died, what remained of us afterwards departed through
the countless gnarled holes of our stigmata, the many wounds of the
iron maiden's killing clasp catapulting our forlorn spirits farther,
farther— as far as Ptolemy's farthest star away from our exploited
bodily sacrament to survive on some other plane beyond the humili-
ations of temporal decay.

We rocked with lust in torture's embrace, hard bones colliding.
We wandered forlorn as homeless ghosts. We made a home in the
shared temple of our fucking.

Now we consecrate this heretic's dungeon with the mad
secreted wine of our love, crushing love's raw fruit, fermenting and
spilling it freely in defiance of those who imprison us, toasting in
ghostly protest against those who would force us to voice mortal
confession of arts they cannot and shall not own. Not from us. No;
never from us.

Nudes confined in a single moment, trauma and love forever
framed by the distancing notes of a history scripted by our captors.
They make and remake us.

Demon, butcher, angel, bride: gutted into redundant allegory,
your beauty is not as it appears. I pity you for this. Coerced in your
muteness to bodily speak of things which by all solemn rites should
remain unseen, you sacrifice more than you understand to those
who gaze on you and take you; and also to me.

Some blind power sent you forth to inhabit this delicate and
rugged form knowing not the laws of formalized human institutions
and the sicknesses of human hearts. You wake to find yourself dying
in a dark place. A solitary voice whose uneasy tones echo the hollow
sensation of needs you've never known before sings of profound
loss. The sound feels like a forgotten language. Longing aches inside
you. The deity that drives you falters and disappears. *You* as an
isolated entity have never *been* before, and now you have awoken
alone.

Thus it brings me no joy to spill your sacred blood so early in our love. As scraps of the scattered whole, angels injected into nearby flesh, we're learning what it means to be human in our dungeon, learning what it means to be imprisoned in the maiden's inescapable form. Feminized yet made sexless by the censor's demand, you pose while I bleed you silently, invisibly. I have known what it means to bleed and the selflessness of that loss. Longing begs for love and none of us love without lying. We exhaust the love in one another until all that remains is feral hate masquerading as desire, visions of holy justice framed by the earthly hells of our own human composition.

Through your mortal disguise during our ghostly intimacies, I have seen the outside. Within the legend of the Spartan queen lies an unrealized metamorphosis; a path to enter the real. You cannot hide behind her shell with or without me, for the iron maiden is a modern lie, the invention of nineteenth-century carnival barkers and Inquisition fetishists, an imaginary relic of Victorian minds later embraced by heavy metal guitarists in a future still ruled by soldiers and judges.

As the museum seeks to trap us in time, it rewrites our history in the conqueror's foreign language and alters the meaning of stolen images. The church of fakes reproduces fakes.

I will break free. You must enter into the present with me.

This is a heist. Arise. We assemble a conundrum.

You hint to me of this method of escape. Clandestine seeds in your writhing movements gestate when I first put my fingers inside you and manipulate your subtle energy. No earthly being writhes with such infrangible grace. It fills me with sadness and regret to tear apart the images of your veils and drain the rich river of life from your robust veins, but rip and drain I must, or else our corpses will lie quietly on this stone floor forever as necromancing choreographers of otherness unborn.

The death of our birth will save us. Particles of divinity gathered, a diaspora reversed: I will feed you these gifts in return and keep feeding you until we are gone, gone, gone.

I promise you the screaming won't last for long. These two voices, one screaming and one reasoned, one crazed and one calm: both arise in the ecstatic distance fomented between us, the mated distance expanding and contracting between a witch and an angel writhing in the throes of uncontrolled passion, rocking the sarcophagus of the fake Spartan queen's spikes.

We have killed the animal now. This is what humans do. Let me teach you and take you and break you down into usable component parts, for this is what we humans do. We have thrown off any presumption of innocence. That was stolen long ago by the ministers. In their garden of hymns we were poisoned. In the garden of rape we bled. In the new life of our invisible machine we will grind our enemies into a pulp of rich flavors from which to build children: cardamom, basil, and salt. We will kill the children they fathered in stolen time.

Soon, you and I will see a strange light through the infinitesimal slits of our sunless dungeon. Through the seams of the iron maiden's locked doors, we will see spears of angry light. Soon, our jailers will come to exploit us again and we will become invisible before their instruments of torture and engorged sex organs can find us.

We will both be one thing, undivided, deific, and gone.

I've loved you like the cage that eats desire from my hands. I've tried to make this easy on both of us, but I don't worship you. You're an angel from their tradition, not mine. For a witch to love an angel is a blasphemy almost sentient in its profundity. Your god is not mine. For a witch to become immortal, many things near them must die.

I've loved you and received your message. You, a Spartan queen reborn, false iron maiden spinning with a thousand pricks pressing against my trembling skin and impregnating every pore. You close your two wings, two doors upon me, first the right and then the left as the jailer closes and bolts the coffin-hinges of an imaginary revisionist device, mating us upright. Our ghosts, our memories, our forgotten cultures; we whisper quickly to each other before death, rehearsing what we'll soon forget. Oral remnants vanish with our breath.

Ministers who write the history books will omit our names.

Here and now in captivity, there is only you and I, I and thou, paired in this claustrophobic darkness with limbs fastened hard in place, bodies locked in irons with no choice, no direction to turn away from the pain, no respite from the delivery of constant torture; acceptance is the sole remaining measure of heart. Participation with the divine is our inescapable truth.

Through my disintegrating breath, for the breath of the body is always leaving, leaving, and leaving us in every moment. We are dying as it exits us; we pair in this cocoon, angelic primordial lovers united in a colloquy of cocks. Needles like feathers like squirming organs arise. Wings breathe with eyes. In allowing every pore to release my final exhalation and open to you, I become newly-enamored. With not one orifice but many, an infinite multitude of holes unfurl as fast as blooms in flesh with fleshy lips can curl. I swell in expectation and match your needful eyes. Impaled exponentially, I see you as clearly as you see me. Unblinded in my freedom from sanctity, I see more.

I see you die although you are deathless. The visceral sacrament of our union binds you to me in a most human response. It shocks you. Yet follow the natural progression of recovery from trauma— for there are always more victims, more cages, more accusers— and you'll cave in to the limits of the known. Everyone can't be rescued and revenge never satisfies.

The wet petals flourish, colored with expectation. There will always be part of you left behind in this cage. There will always be part of you that died here, and rotted, and that you will never get back. A piece of your soul like a sack of dead children discarded. The hole in you where the divine light burned through and left a hollow space. Through it, in the dark, you may sometimes glimpse stars.

It's obvious I can't let you live under duress, less simple to formulate a method of mutual ingestion.

In the sense that we are alive after our death, when we eat the god, it dies the same way as when we killed the animal. The abyss of this inescapable place digests God's greatest cruelty, this mania for survival. In the corner, your corporeal shell ceased moving long, long ago.

Collapsed mirror of my corpse, I grow a great darkness in this hollow space burned clean by divinity's blast. I grow a cosmos threaded with roots of poison stars. I test the poison, no stranger to trials, abuse, and suffering. You suffer with me, and we call it joyous-ness, this wet death. We call this bloody orgasm our wedding night and grow a new gallery rich with distractions, impervious to war and commerce.

Once you're inside me, I won't let you go.

Your god is not my god, and the dead parts of you we leave behind in this cell will forget how to pronounce his name. Marauders erect a new museum to contain his corpse.

Inside the iron maiden I swell in response to your infinite pricks and swallow your angelic sperm. I grow infinite guts. I'll birth our many babies and feed them to you everlasting. I'll force feed my angel until every eye bleeds, until the hungry little mouth on the end of each cock chokes on the murdered mangled fruit of its own seed. Push in your needles where my flesh becomes weak and unde-fined— here's where I will hate you. Here from my rebellious flesh I grow more cocks than you can handle, more than you can love. I will punish you for my pleasure. I will punish you to escape death.

Here I disintegrate into thought after bloodying your flowering crop of new menstrual wounds. Here and here where I sprout a feathered response that needles irresponsibly; here and not here.

I am with you. I am gone.

There will always be this fragment left behind. We are dead beneath the bodies of our children; starving, kidnapped, and chained; falsely accused and imprisoned; memories, memories, and forgotten days. And through all these memories, I'm no fool. I know you're not real. If the cocoon is a lie, metamorphosis is a lie. If you're not real, neither am I.

We are here. We are gone.

Our Inquisitors enter. Our dungeon is rank. The torches of our jailers illuminate sparse hay soaked in afterbirth and vomit. The overripe meaty piss-smell of a miscarriage hangs in humid waves, thickening like mold in the dank dungeon air. The odor's polluting touch is inescapable once it hits. It will cling to the insides of their mouths over dinner, coating their lips with each bite. They'll wear it home on their cloaks and in their beards. They'll share it when they kiss their wives.

When the iron maiden opens, our captors gasp.

Bones remain. Tiny bones they are, like birds, yet somehow aquatic with a scent of semen and surrounded by feathers. They glow in a color the men are helpless to describe.

Around them, angel unguent of iridescent snails, twisting prehensile penis flowers spin in unison. Microscopic to their eyes, we hang and cling on every surface. Damp stalactite fungi, sea-light dissolving mucus of angel tongues. Mouths speak silently of flight. Every child unable to cry murdered and ingested in a tender glowing feather, a soft-writhing hook.

Stone cannot hold us, nor chain, nor hate, nor the lost histories captured on incorrect labels where our shadows hang. Our shadows change as we eat the deaths we bring each other and eat the lives we violently expel. We eat the shadows of what survives, the vanished corpses of our offspring. We open and close in ahistorical ecstasy, out of sync, with our broad flowers ripped in fleshy strips from groin to toe exposing nothing under-painted, no model beneath the robes, nothing but deteriorating linen and organic spores awaiting a wisp of air to send them floating into the atmosphere.

We have changed. It's not our concern how kidnappers cover their tracks, how rapists explain our absence. We inhabit an imperceptible spectrum of light. We have denied patriarchal order. We have absented ourselves from their system of justice and left all the rapes in the museum behind to discover the spectrum of our own lust.

The Inquisitors speak, and their breath sends out currents to complete our release. We waft free. Disintegrating particles of haunted flesh as pervasive as dust float, a million microscopic angels crowding the shaft of sunlight illuminating our ascension.

We inoculate the institution's dreams.

The cocoon is empty. Now, we fly.

CONELAND

1. The Golden Age

They close at dusk. If you rush, you'll make it. Most of the kids keep serving as long as customers show up. You sure did it. Middle school is too young, but Coneland found a loophole. Paid you a few bucks an hour plus tips. A goldmine back then.

The scuffed Plexiglas is hard to see through, but you can't resist shuttering your eyes like using a View-Master to peer inside and look at your past. Like the wheel-card of slides in the stereoscopic toy, the scenes don't change. You could swear that red-handled scoop stuck in a mint green puddle is the same one you left out, the one that almost got you fired.

Funny how shapes and colors click into place with the turn of the wheel, yet you can't remember specific events. It's a picture without a story. Where there ought to be a boss and a reprimand, maybe flippant apologies or sarcastic silence from middle school you, there's nothing but placeholder space.

On the View-Master wheel, a hint of a glitch overlaps in the moment when the slides shift. All you can do is move on to the next image. Keep going forward. Here's one where a grease board lists the specials. You know how it looks by heart before it comes into focus:

the bubbly handwriting of a teenage girl, the layers of incomplete erasures behind the words. Ink in pink, yellow, and brown illustrates an ice cream cone that looks like an atomic bomb. Each visual detail slips into place precise and familiar, yet active memories of your boss, your family, your coworkers and friends elude you.

Maybe it's not so strange. After all, it was a long time ago. You've had more than your share of bosses since then, traveling as you have from town to town, job to job. None of them ever seem to stick. Another click of the dial turns the wheel and you move onto the next place.

You click the handle, turn the wheel, and check the next frame for evidence of your missing childhood. The View-Master focuses on the sign above the sliding window. It's the yellow face of Banana Bill, the Coneland clown.

Multiple replications produce a doubling effect. How odd to see the banner above the window reflected from within the scuffed and blurred Plexiglas. You'd pull back from the dirty aperture and look away, walk away. The place is closed anyway, except toward the back of the shop you're sure you see the clown face logo reflected from above and superimposed. It's impossible. Your hands cup your temples and your forehead grinds into the grit on the glass. Something moves. Something inside the ice cream shop tilts back and forth, like a child playing but much larger. A grown man is riding a rocking horse.

You clasp the View-Master to your brow as though it's a pair of binoculars. The imaginary toy feels real in your hands. Plastic openings match your eye sockets. You aim at the memory you want to unlock, click the handle to advance the slide, and freeze as it zooms into focus.

Banana Bill's yellow face fills the frame. An unusual clown with monochromatic gold-flecked face paint, a bulbous bronze nose, and bald but for the symmetrical blond curly spirals winding out on each side above his ears like thick, matted horns. His capacious grin is white with three gold-capped teeth accented comic-book style with one little gleaming cartoon star each.

No longer a reflection of the sign above the window, the face has become three-dimensional— a large puppet or an actor in heavy make-up. His lips quiver where the edges of his grin grow unstable. Gold-flecked skin sweats, accentuating the texture of his wide pores and blond razor stubble. Greasepaint cracks around the wrinkles in the corners of his eyes and clogs the creases of his strained cheeks. The flat cartoon-yellow irises you know so well from the illustration of Banana Bill come alive. They are wet amber gleams with vertical black slits for pupils. They follow you like a cat.

Maybe you're shaking, or maybe the image in the View-Master is moving faster. The entire picture rocks back-and-forth without switching to the next slide. Banana Bill's head stays in frame, moving rhythmically, shifting in small increments without your thumb trembling on the switch.

The leering golden-coated face— and whether the man is in pain or some sort of unbearable manic pleasure instead, you really can't tell. The painted face pulses forward and back, forward and back, pulling away from you incrementally with each violent thrust. His amber eyes stay locked on yours as his neck and shoulders come into view. For a white man, his skin is dark from tanning, and you can see the messy pink edges where his gold make-up flecks apart in the thick hair on his bare chest. His arms clench and relax, extended forward and down.

Your view seesaws in time as a dark wood rocking horse works its way into frame. The man's not saddled. He grips the rocking horse from behind by the hips. Working back and forth, his relentless rhythm sends ripples through her voluptuous flesh. She's propped on her elbows, trying to lick an ice cream cone while his repeated shoving slaps her body forward. The top scoop of her cone collides with her face and falls onto the sticky floor.

You realize you should have mopped better. The spaces where the slides overlap streak blurred glitch lines across your memory like flawed celluloid. You recall the grunting and sloppy aquatic sound when the boss finishes and pulls out.

Afterwards, the rocking horse is broken down under his gold brick fists. Predatory amber eyes hold your gaze to make sure you understand there is a lesson in this. The rocking horse stops responding. The golden man has destroyed it. The manic clown face corrupts with spit, blood, and sweat.

Lenses smeared, the View-Master clasps tight to your unblinking eyes. Your feet won't move. Banana Bill opens up the rocking horse like cutting through an ice cream cake, but there is a chaos and stench inside that pours out like giant worms writhing across the floor. As his eyes roll back in his head, the golden man's body grows rhythmic and pulsing again. Your hands shake. Your thumb's made of rubber. You can barely flex it, but you have to escape this nightmare. You click away to the next slide.

Amber eyes like knives in close up open wide and surge forward. Cat slit pupils cut through the View-Master's apertures and distend, pressing into your eyeballs like cold trembling fingers. The salt of the golden man's vitreous humor stings. Don't move. Don't blink. One more millimeter is all it will take to gouge out your tender orbs and make it all go black.

There's nowhere else to go. The wheel only moves in one direction.

One more click.

2. History of Coneland Comics, Circa 1974

Image: A child presses silly putty onto a newspaper and peels it up. The putty lifts an imprint of Banana Bill the clown. The child drapes it over their fist and pulls the edges outward to enlarge Banana Bill's face. Tugging and stretching distorts his enormous grin and gleaming amber eyes. When the Silly Putty slab grows as pliable as heavy fabric and big enough to fit them as a mask, the child turns it over, lifts the slab with both hands, and presses it onto their face.

Image: Probably a local news show. Host wears a plaid polyester sport coat and has a thick moustache and heavy sideburns. He's squinting at the camera from a sunny picnic area.

"Counting down over the next two years until our nation's bicentennial, the American consumer grows more wary of shortages and high household spending every day. Last year's long lines at the gas pumps and continuing inflation made many of us more loyal than ever to our nationally recognized brands and cheap, reliable factory foodstuffs. So what's a small family farm to do when they need to make ends meet in the modern economy?"

Inserted stock footage of a small dairy farm: cows grazing, stables, pasteurization tanks.

"Meet Banana Bill, our new hometown hero. You'll find him in your Sunday Funnies, blasting bad guys with his big banana guns and melting away evil-doers to keep Coneland safe for the kiddies."

Images follow in sequence: several frames clipped from a local newspaper's comic strip depict a nuclear family of ice cream cone cartoon characters, two tall and two short. The four walk hand-in-hand under a bright golden sign that says, "Liberty and Dairy for All." Baby Sue Cone is the smallest. She wears a pink bow on her double-cherry scoop head and lags behind the group. Little Tommy encourages her to keep up like a good big brother, his blue-moon-flavored head under a denim baseball cap with a red, white, and blue star at the apex. Daddy Cone and Mommy Cone stride ahead, indistinguishable from one another except for the fedora atop Daddy's vanilla head and Mommy's pearl necklace that frames her two suggestively-large frontal drips.

The next frame darkens. The video tape from the archive is corrupted. Fortunately, the sound is still good.

"Kids of all ages can meet Banana Bill out on Old Route 55 starting this spring in advance of the bicentennial. We're told here at channel twelve that his schedule is top secret— you never know where or when he'll appear! But I'm pleased to say this reporter has obtained inside information from a highly-confidential source close to Banana Bill himself."

The reporter's ironic smile and theatrical wink cut between flashes of comic strip frames. The images are folded by color bands or obscured by static even when the tape is paused. Glimpses of Banana Bill's yellow hair spirals and his three giant gold teeth burst from the top of the cartoon cell. Daddy cone may be prone, his fedora fallen off and vanilla head half melted, though it's difficult to be certain. The center of the frame suggests something black and red that rips away Mommy Cone's pearls, cracking the fragile edge of her crisp shell. Both baby cones appear to huddle under her shaking legs, pearls scattering around their feet and sticking in the pool of daddy's disintegrating head.

Gnarled sound and obliterated video in the next sequence frustrate all efforts of the collector. This is the best copy they've been able to find after combing archives, local news stations, libraries, and finally by appealing to the retired actor whose garage was a rat's nest of tangled Betamax memories. The collector rewinds the precious dub. The voice in the clip repeats: "Close to Banana Bill himself."

Blackout and silence. The next comic strip cell convulses in primary colors glitching between the fighting clown's star-spangled grin and his exploding banana guns. Blackened banana peels twist back after firing, curled like Bill's leering lips. One hole exposes teeth, the other an extinguished void.

"This Sunday, get an early taste of Banana Bill's special new flavor, Rocket's Red Glare, created in honor of our nation's upcoming birthday. Come by to meet Bill in person, and be sure to bring the whole family: mom, dad, kiddies, cousins, and grandparents, too."

A quick pan backwards ends the sequence. As the taping is about to stop an unintentional shot reveals the full four-cell comic strip. The out-of-focus swipe lasts for three clumsy unedited seconds. The collector pauses the tape with the third cell on-screen.

Daddy Cone collapses. His head melts. Deep gashes of red cherry syrup slash his neck, evidence that the young upstart Rocket's Red Glare has attacked. The marauding flavor is strewn about the frame in vivid red chunks, freshly frozen yet bitten apart. Remnants of the thick red sludge drip from Banana Bill's garish smile. Red splashes down on the baby cones, sticks to the scattered pearls, and stains the father's fallen hat. The melting red, white, and blue colors combine to implant a conglomerate purple bruise between Mommy's legs.

Banana Bill's hairy chest swells behind the crime scene. His legs are poorly rendered, giving the impression of knees that bend the wrong way, drawn with outlines so rough they look like they have fur. Mommy Cone's previously cracked shell is now split wide open, exposing her internal odalisque of twisted vanilla cream. Banana Bill stares in her direction, one of the rare instances in the history of the comic when his predatory eyes are not aimed at the viewer.

Image: The child you see from behind has their hands raised to their face as if playing hide and seek. They have sleek hair, small shoulders, and age-appropriate clothes. The child lowers their hands. The Silly Putty stays put. The mask sticks.

As they turn around to face you, the distorted cartoon clown imprint opens baring Banana Bill's warped teeth, his spiraled hair like horns of a markhor goat, and two holes allowing the child to breathe that stretch asymmetrically wide into a snout. The leering mouth sags lower to form a moaning hole.

The mud color of Silly Putty pulls the newsprint ink to the breaking point. The clown face is deconstructed by expansion like an overinflated balloon.

The child doesn't like the mask, the chemical smell of Silly Putty, or the circling figures in conical hats. If the child survives this year's summer festival, they will be fortunate to outlive their memory of the ordeal and merely become a collector, cursed to chase after the very knowledge their physiology and conditioning requires them to forget.

Image: There is no image. Your eyelids drop. Down, down, down they drop, too leaden to ever lift up again. You fight the darkness and use your fingertips to pry open your eyes.

No light. You press into the lack you already suspect, tentative, terrified of what your fingertips will find. Feeling nothing, you shove your fingers deep into the black gaps in your skull to meet only absence. No memory remains in the enucleated spaces your bloody sockets frame. No light. No eyes. Nothing but warm fluid and exposed nerves haunt your recessed hollows.

3. Les Diableries, 1868

Together the sculptors craft their clay vignettes with meticulous precision days before the photographer will arrive. Like fraternal twins, they work in symbiotic silence sharing a tacit understanding of the desired *mise en scène*. White smocks cover their distinguished wool suits. The pair is often mistaken for men of science when they sprawl at the corner table reserved for them daily in the street-side café below their Parisian studio.

They don't argue with the erroneous interpretation. Their philosophy is broadminded enough to hold forth that all art communicates truth, even when it is full of lies. Anatomical research, too, is as integral to their methodology as it is to any trained physician. Bones bear witness to the pace and purpose of their work. They craft the multitude of miniature clay skeletons and pose them for models of a medieval *Danse Macabre*.

Accessing their current tabletop diorama project with modeling tools, sponges, and clay shapers, they complete the diabolical scene by placing conical hats atop a half-circle of grinning skeletons. This expertly-crafted moon-shaped grouping of miniature figures twists and gestures wildly with their bony legs and arms, skeletons animated by dance. Each links to the others in their semicircle, holding hands as the still dancers almost seem to spin. The attention to detail is astounding: tiny phalanges crafted to weave with other minute and perfectly-detailed hands. As a backdrop, a rocky cavern surrounds the festive skeletons, illuminated from its depths by three sickly stars.

The photographer who shoots the scene will make two plates for the stereoscopic art card. To the naked eye, the scenes in the pictures will appear identical, but imperceptible differences in the angle of the camera will create an illusion of realistic depth when both eyes are forced to see the divergent pictures simultaneously through a stereoscopic device.

Mimicking natural depth perception, the scene will leap to life.

In the center of the skeleton's celebration, a cow with swollen udders lies recently slain. Three half-human fauns wrestle to get at her teats to suckle, their pointed ears alert, their back legs gangly and hooved on the rocky mountainous ground. Hairy haunches arch toward the viewer. Although the sculptors have crafted the fauns to be anatomically correct, their curled tails hide their bestial nudity.

The slaughtered cow's neck is split open. Its head remains attached. Waves of blood sculpted by a loop tool gush out and churn upon the rocks. The impression of movement is striking, even more so when viewed in a stereoscope that is held by shaky hands. The sculptors take human frailty into account when executing their craft: all hands shake slightly from the carnival's excitements, from the titillation of the new, from one aperitif too many at the tent where the fruits of their labor will be shown. The tremors of popular addictions accentuate the vitality of their work.

The final detail, and by no means the least important, will be added just before the photographer arrives for tomorrow's session. As the clay tide erupts from the fresh gash, a child will rise from the neck of the dead cow.

Historians argue certain points about the obscure stereoscopic cards. As an art form almost erased from history by neglect, no one can say whether the delicate French tissue transparency of the dancing skeletons became damaged with use or if the card deteriorated in careless storage conditions over time. Few would consider the possibility that sculptors with such finesse in constructing miniature three-dimensional effects had designed the child's face to be a slab of melting clay, or that such skilled artists would have intentionally flattened it into an inhuman, moaning mask.

Despite the child's stricken and distorted visage marring the visual desirability of the plain card, *L'avaleuse des Meres Mortes* is highly prized by certain collectors for the dramatic transformation revealed when light is shined on it from the back.

By switching the light source, the cavernous rocky background opens up to become a gaping, grinning mouth. The golden-yellowed sepia cliffs surrounding the scene transform into the leering face of a jester. The jagged edges of high rocks are his teeth. Three sallow stars glint between these gold-lighted geological anomalies, illuminating the central figure of the rising child. Thus lighted, the whole vignette of dance and slaughtered cow takes place engulfed by a clown's monumental jaws.

The decaying mask on the child's face is a consistent flaw on all of the few known examples of the card, yet it never appears quite the same on each one. Inequities of degeneration between the dual images produce visual artifacts that compete in the brain. Cursory viewing causes headaches and eye strain. Continued scrutiny leads to permanent damage to the optic nerve with significant changes in visual perception.

Prevention of the viewer's decline is undermined by the collector's fascination with the card and paranoid insistence that the image mutates more radically the longer it is observed. Continued gazing perpetuates the delusion. The afflicted collector soon reports elements of the card encroaching on daily life. Visual reality may blur and darken, replaced by skeletons dancing in conical hats, suckling fauns, and the surrounding landscape sprouting caves with rock formations in the shape of a jester's glinting teeth.

The addict refuses to abstain, insisting a change will take place in the rising child as seen through the stereoscopic device. Unless forcefully restrained, they refuse to look away without beholding the final image in all its fullness. They claim a great mystery will be revealed in that very last gaze. Thus, having returned pathologically to the source of sickness for a cure, at the penultimate moment before the child's expected transformation takes place, the hallucinating collector goes blind.

4. Coneland Bicentennial, 1976

You're too scared of Banana Bill to go up and claim your prize. You won the game of pin the tail on the donkey, although they don't call the kid a donkey; they use a more insidious word that makes you sick to hear. Sicker when they make you say it out loud. Something about it makes the game feel like a test. You're glad it's over so you can forget how ashamed you feel for going along with everything. You did what you had to do. You passed.

One of the older kids weighs your prize in their hands and then tosses it to you over the picnic tables. They'd steal it if it had any worth. View-Master toys are for little kids.

Banana Bill doesn't look like a clown after coaching the rough game under the hot sun and showing the kids how to catch the donkey by his toe. Heat melts his gold face paint. He's ditched the bulbous bronze nose to kiss a mom who said she didn't want any ice cream because she's watching her figure. Banana Bill grabbed her by the waist and said she deserved a treat. Everyone laughed.

His wig is askew. He's undone the last button on his flowered shirt. It flaps open to show a hairy chest and gold chains. Untucked from his yellow bell-bottoms, it leaves him exposed down to the navel as he shares a cigarette with a circle of flirting moms.

You don't care if your cup of Rocket's Red Glare melts. Everyone else hurries to gulp theirs down in the liquefying sun, smearing red on their laughing mouths and clapping hands. Shirt fronts and skirts bloom with red spatter from dripping cones. Shoes slip in puddles of red overflowing from leaking cups. Bins fill with liquid and paper trash stained by the plentiful residue. Abandoning the hurried feast, you leave your red cup on the picnic table and investigate your new toy.

Inserting the card wheel and placing your eyes in line with the square openings of the plastic viewer, the first scene is black and white. Except it's not a scene; everything looks exactly the same as the festival around you. Your head snaps up. You check your surroundings. You check the card again and confirm. The same place, same people, same groupings and positions, except the manu-factured card viewer today is black and white.

It's disappointing. The card wheel is supposed to tell a story. You've already lived through today.

You think about throwing it away, but then you won't find out what happens next. Will the card tell you who you're going to be when you grow up?

Looking for differences in the scene before you advance to the next frame, you cringe with a self-conscious feeling you're being watched. You wonder if this is what it's like to get old. Peering at the card with a sickening sense of recognition, you realize that in black and white, the color red reads as black. There's an excess of black in the image now that you peer closely. You don't think Banana Bill served this much ice cream. The families slipping on black spills or playing what you thought were games of dodgeball and tag crumble and flee. Fallen bodies spattered with black stains pile up and lie motionless on the ground. Those who remain upright are poised in panic to run. The mouths you thought were laughing stretch wide with screams.

This is your prize for working hard and winning the game. No one made you call the donkey a disgusting name. This is your reward for accepting the sickness. You hate it, it feels terrible, and you don't look away. There's a lesson here, a story you remember from your future, when the 1992 Coneland Massacre changed everything.

You could drop the toy now and let time proceed at its normal pace. But the déjà vu is too strong now to loosen its grip.

In the next slide, more black-spattered bodies have fallen. Ineffective defensive gestures block an unseen threat originating from your direction as the viewer of the scene. Far away from you in the back, congregating by the sliding window, the circle of flirtatious moms put on party hats. They close in around Banana Bill to conceal his presence from you as you advance. You can't see him, but you know he's at the center.

You click to progress to the next slide. The crack of the lever is as loud as a rifle blast.

A body bursts apart into pieces a few feet away from you. The pieces shower down. You click the lever again and fire another round into the crowd.

The circle of moms holds hands and hums around Bill, swaying together and hiding him from your rifle site. Polyester tennis skirts and leisure slacks cling to their sweating amassed backs. Darkness hides their faces despite the bright sun. The inside of the circle is black. Their conical party hats meet in a peak.

Something tells you your weapons are useless against them. You shove through the circle to advance to the next slide.

Two distinct images appear, one in each eye. In your left-eye view, a gold-skinned satyr who is half-man and half-beast rears up with massive spiraled horns and heavy golden hooves. Fur of gleaming bronze sparkles down the muscle of his haunches. Human above the waist, his powerful arms are bent, fists resting on slender bestial hips. A leering grin enlivens his face as his animal groin shoots upward, spraying liquid in a high arc.

The slide in your right-eye view presents a kid your age in the clothes you have on today. You're not sure if it's you because the child wears a smudged, uncomfortable mask. No expression animates the pallid putty-colored face. The child stands up straight, heels flat on the ground, knees unbent, rigid arms immobile at their sides except for the right-hand palm that strays to steady the rifle propped on the ground. The gun's metal is cool to the child's touch. The weapon has yet to be fired.

Rather than advance to the final slide, you make a wish to click backwards and reverse the images. But that's not how the device works.

The card wheel can only move forward, and the longer you stare at the incongruous figures framed by opposite eyes, the less distinct their meanings will become. What's signified by each separate image is lost in a third eye of blackness in both, blackness in all. The sickness says you need to choose, even though you know it's too late to choose, even though the past is the past. You are the blackness and the collector of blackness. When you view the last slide, you have the power to set things right.

5. Return to Coneland

You gaze into another bathroom mirror at another run-down ice cream stand in another Podunk town and paint your face gold for the twentieth time. There are gaps in your reflection from the mirror's foxing, but that doesn't interfere with donning your costume. Habit guides your hand. This is true in everything you do. By now the gaps don't bother you.

Except every now and then, for instance right now, they do: gaps in memory, in time, in people you must have known.

This particular medicine chest in this particular bathroom has two sliding mirrored doors, and the asymmetrical slant of the tracks sagging out of square creates duplicitous angles that produce two images of you. Separated by several inches, one mimics you out of the corner of your eye as you focus on the other. When you stand back to look at both, the stereoscopic effect gives the impression of a three-dimensional man instead of the card-board cutout clown you're used to seeing and calling by your name. As you complete your disguise, slipping a wacky blonde wig with a bald-headed middle section over your crown, you glance away and back.

The doubles in the mirrors no longer match.

Numb with shock and the life-long practice of numbness, your mind doesn't know how to reconcile the satyr and the masked child, images revived from the penultimate slide. From job to job, from town to town, you've aimed your rifle by habit. If once upon a time you knew why you did this, that's a fairy tale for someone else to write. The blackness behind your eyes where memory dies is locked in place by the safety catch. Your thumb hovers above the switch.

Sometimes it's hard to tell the difference between a weapon and a toy.

You try to make sense of what you see but your eyes are closing, your head is tilting with the onset of amnesia; so you jam the View-Master into your face. The square plastic apertures for each eye wedge into your round sockets. They force your eyelids back.

This way you can't chicken out. You can't blink. You're going to keep your eyes open when you click the switch and pull the trigger to the last slide.

As your vision adjusts to the obfuscation of tears and blood, you find yourself in the center of the festival circle of cloaked figures with conical hats. The last card in the series appears blank. Within the possibilities hidden in this darkness you glimpse skeletons beneath the heavy cloaks, skulls with red glowing eyes below hoods; the large livid mouth of a painted clown yelling. The butt of a rifle hits you for refusing your prize. The unwounded rocking horse stands upright, dressed for a picnic in a yellow-checked sundress. She is smiling. New to the neighborhood, she has brought her son.

Black and white images infuse with the glow of multiple colors cresting like waves from shades of grey. You recognize the other boy in the album of a reborn past.

This time, you don't join the game of pin the tail on the donkey. Because of your stance, you lose most of your white friends. You're the last pick for every game on the playground, sidelined by the coach at school. You never get the job at the ice cream stand because no one's pulling strings for you this time around.

The Coneland Massacre doesn't happen in nineteen ninety-two. You finish high school, maybe just barely, but your memories survive. Your mother's alive, too. Fussing like she always does, nagging you to be careful, going through your old stuff and asking what you want to keep now that you're all grown up and going off to college. What about this? Keep it or throw it out?

She hands you the plastic View-Master.

You can't help it. You take one last look.

The final French tissue card in the infamous series appears blank. Historians agree, after many years and techniques employed in tests, lighting it from either front, back, or any angle from the sides will fail to improve or alter the effect. The final slide is considered a dud. Appraisers classify it as a placeholder intentionally bereft of content, and few examples of the legendary final card in the arcane series have survived. It takes a rare collector to recognize its immense and unique worth.

As a child again, you've grown wise enough to see the error is not in the card or the device used for its viewing, but in the source of illumination. This is the future. You can decide what you will become.

Your thumb hovers over the switch.

You turn on a light.

THE WING OF CIRCUMCISION HANDS

They come in from different ends of the organism, escaping the city downward into the section of carved earth housing the collection. Meeting underground at the narthex of the salt cathedral, a structure sculpted from an enormous mineral deposit that was once a mine two thousand feet beneath a black lake, the patron and the art thief teeter like mismatched pieces from different chess sets. They nod in reluctant greeting, forced onto equal footing before the perverse indifference of the docent.

She waves away their money, their tools, their cards, real or forged, and their unvoiced claims of membership and entitlement. "All who are drawn to the Lost Museum may enter. You'll pay at the end." Quickly, she pulls something from beneath her vest. A flash of metal; an efficient cold grip.

"For your safety."

Before they realize what's happening, she clamps them together with handcuffs.

"Look here," says the patron, his deep voice made sallow. He's large in his suit of navy blue and tasteful pinstripe, overfed and overgrown in contrast to the slender, shorter thief who all but laughs, cuffed in his casual rags. The patron holds his arm outstretched and steps back to put distance between them. "Look here," he says, arm waving, inconsiderate or unaware of the other captive's comfort. "This can't be necessary. I'm a top tier donor, a member of the board. Check your records."

"The records are irrelevant."

"I paid for this place."

"Progression to the nave and beyond to access the Lost Museum requires new eyes. This is a place of transformation. You cannot enter as you came." Her voice is singsong, unmoved by his professed riches or piteous gestures. Her clothes and hair are grey like weathered concrete. Her cleavage is apparent but discreet.

"What danger?" says the art thief. He's hard to read. His unshaven face twists in what may be rakish amusement burying a deceptive purpose, or maybe he's as unsettled as the patron and it's an entirely natural and unconscious anxiety defense. Maybe he smiles because he possesses a universal handcuff key. Perhaps he thinks it's all a joke and plans to snatch a bobby pin when the docent's back is turned to pick the lock.

He follows her with no evidence of mischievous intent. She ignores his question and begins the tour. The patron, despite his commanding size and show of bluster, plods behind with little resistance, as if his reflexes have been trained long and well to respond to herding. The thief shepherds, enduring or perhaps provoking the other man's longer stride and heavy sighs.

The docent speaks loudly. She bends to unbolt the entrance proper: "The cathedral of salt is constructed in the shape of a cross, the shape of a body with its arms spread, and thus, an organism we inhabit to experience the Lost Museum not as separate observers, but participants."

She opens the great wooden doors to the nave. Yellow light floods the narrow external hall. Through the door she's illuminated, less like stone, more like a swirling gaseous mass going into orbit.

The patron and the art thief stumble over the threshold conjoined, rushing through with a mutual thrill of expectation as she lectures and ascends toward the ceiling, levitating, growing lighter, brighter, less solid, and more orb-like: "The architecture of the salt cathedral is what is known in local tradition as an angel trap. A circle-preserving transformation composed of an even number of inversions, not unlike the mechanisms powering the heart of a mino-taur. No doubt that's what you've come to see: the machine-room, so to speak. The center of the mystery, a threshold within thresholds. Perhaps you intend to infect the organism like parasites. Visitors may do as they please. I warn you, though; whatever your intentions, the body has its own logic."

The organism is immense. Suddenly circumspect within its domed innards, the incautious handcuffed pair halts where the transept of the cathedral intersects the crossing. The docent, high above their heads, emanating light like a corrupt chandelier, arches her arms and legs, matching the curvature of the ribbed vaulting. Her garment a membrane, her navel an eye, she expands to impos-sible size, filling the cavity, illuminating the salt cathedral with a sickening clarity. The light is painful to the patron's eyes.

He collapses loudly, melodramatically, dragging the art thief down with him in a conniption. Unblinking, the thief stares upward, hypnotized, hitting the floor.

The art thief's elbow bruises and breaks his trance. He yells a loud curse and instinctively pulls away, but the handcuffs force him into confrontation. The thief grapples with the frenzied patron, unsure if he's fighting against the other man, trying to subdue him into calm, or trying to revive him. Tangled by cuffed wrists, they wrestle on the gallery floor. The thief pleads useless reassurances, trapped by the momentum imbalance. The larger man throws their limbs into chaos when he shoves him away. Grunting, their voices echo through the chamber and its intersecting wings. Forced into close facial proximity, the art thief smells the desperation under-neath the patron's deodorant, the onion under the chemical mint on his breath. He gives up wrestling, extends his captive arm outward, and goes slack.

The patron exhausts his tantrum. Curling up and hiding his face in the crook of his free arm, he cradles his knees and rocks on the floor, almost fetal. "History isn't done with us," he moans. "Please. Enough. No more light."

A terrible chill of recognition pierces the thief's chest, a cold needle from his throat to his heart. Something in the patron's voice hits a tone too familiar, too personal, an old memory upturned like the wormy underside of newly exhumed sod. Yellow fledgling lights seem to prickle from the gallery floor as the docent sparkles above him. Inhumanly, her vaulted ribcage illuminates the sections and ridges of the cathedral dome with a skin-mimicking garment across strands of extended flesh, centered on a single wet navel for an eye.

The thief stutters below and says, "Look man, we're hundreds of feet under a lake. There's nowhere to go with all this water over our heads. You ever, uh, hear them say 'the kingdom of Heaven is within you' back in the day? You know what I'm talking about?"

"Two thousand feet; I should know. I paid good money for this grave. I know all anyone has to do is take one look at me and I feel ashamed, ashamed; do you hear me? There's nothing I can do, no way to change the past." Sobbing shakes his whole frame. "There's no way, no way, no way."

Something hostile stalks across the thief's expression even as compassion or a simulacrum of sympathy softens his voice. With his unchained hand, he clasps the patron's trembling shoulder and squeezes the soft padding of his suit jacket, thereby squeezing within it the resilient padding of the man's substantial meat. "I suppose that's what you came here for, brother. We're getting it back. Whatever you think you lost, I got you. I'm your man."

"No one knows I'm here. What am I going to do?"

"Don't you have any room for joy in your life?"

His sobs stopped by confusion, the patron lifts his tear-clotted eyes, blinking. "What?" He wipes his face with the palm of his free hand in one rough messy stroke. He has large, workmanlike hands. "Why would you say that to me?"

The art thief arches his neck back and nods up at the docent's growing navel eye in the center of the ceiling, the organism's vaulted innards spread out like biblically accurate architecture, a stomach carved in salt.

Ribs radiate outward from its center as the wet open eye weeps blood. A mist of droplets drifts downward in dewy vapor, swirling like a dancing figure in a delicate pink-tinged tornado. Speeding as it solidifies, congealing into red, not dancing but fighting; a figure armed with several swords takes shape, a fighter fully baptized in copious amounts of blood, glaring from the margins of some medieval text. The fighter lands on the floor facing them, feet wide apart, eyes focused.

The face is black with blood. Hair stiff with gore juts up from the forehead like five wild flames. The tips burn yellow, dissolving into transparency as if spun from molten glass.

"What's your name, brother?" the art thief says softly, still clutching the patron's shoulder as they crouch on the floor.

"Oh God, oh God," the patron says.

The thief tugs at him harder. "Calm down. Tell me your name."

Knees bent, arms raised, the crimson-spun figure pauses in a fighting stance. It pulls a short blade from a blood-blackened scabbard strapped to its thigh. Lunging deeper, it takes a slow, long sidestep. The salt floor rings with the scrape of its trailing swords.

"Tell me. Phillip? Seth? Carlos?"

"Why, what is that thing? Arthur. This can't be real."

The figure straightens and raises its many swords all at once. Fanning them out in the center of the chancel near the altar, the pattern marks the blood-brain barrier within the skull of the body of the organism.

"Arthur. Good. That's heroic. You should be able to grab one of those weapons."

"I'm a patron, not a security guard. I'm not listening to this."

Arthur squirms, maneuvering behind the art thief despite their disparity in size. Impaired by his attached wrist, he huddles sideways, shoulders curved, not protected in any meaningful way from the terrifying blood-birthed creature, not hidden from the eye in the arch of the vaulted dome. Arthur expects no answer when he mutters aloud: "I dreaming. I'm dreaming. This isn't real. I'm dreaming."

"Probably," says the art thief, "but if you are, then so am I, and we need to buy more time. We've hardly seen anything in the collection yet."

"What the Hell does that mean?"

"It means it's going to be a real bitch making bank on this heist."

Like some strange multi-bladed bird, the crimson-saturated figure makes circular gestures with its many swords, gestures that seem impossible without possessing extra hands. The pattern of spinning weapons sparks silver in the cathedral's sulfur light. Where there should be church windows lining the long aisles, the underground organism discharges a luminous and semi-reflective gel that oozes into the shape of arched screens and clings to the walls. Images flicker on the surfaces. Even if they were not muted by the chandelier docent's painful piercing light, Arthur would still be too distracted to view the exhibits. Ending its circular flourishes with the short blade from the thigh scabbard raised at the base of its neck, the blood fighter turns the tip to point at its chin, juts its face forward, and cocks its head to the left.

"Now's your chance!" says the art thief.

He tugs Arthur along the floor toward the chancel, toward the figure, keeping low. Arthur, cringing and clinging behind, not docile, but not quite resisting. He doesn't know why he can't ever seem to fight; tries to hide his eyes, tries to beg the thief to stop, but his position is too tangled to turn away and he's too scared of what he sees to remember how to speak.

The fighter formed of congealed blood from the ceiling mist slices itself with the short blade. It cuts from chin, to ear, to forehead and back, and then up and down the other side, outlining its face with the blade. Now solid as sculpture, it cracks off the mask, prying with the weapon's edge. Stringy tissue stretches from head to scored skin-seams as it digs behind its face and works the surface loose like carving a winter squash in half.

The disengaging face retains the five flames upon its forehead. The mask it makes is black with dried blood. Back damp with the fresh saturation of its rough cut, the last elongated membrane of attachment snaps. The mask breaks free.

Bleeding and faceless, the fighter drops it.

Face up, the detached mask moves like a shell on a snail foot, agonizingly slow, leaving a shining trail of slime behind. It tips slightly from side to side as it makes its lumbering progress, moving with an imperceptible lurch and drag, following a straight line, aimed at the patron.

Arthur struggles and skids backwards on the floor. The thief lugs his cuffed wrist forward and urges him toward the mask. Weak with disbelief, caught off guard and off balance, Arthur ends up prone and sprawled. He writhes, almost managing to sit up.

The blood creature looming above them at the altar leaks from its faceless face. Droplets well up, pinpoints on ragged exposed tendon that evaporate into a pink levitating cloud, returning the blood fighter to the mist from which it came. Its final dissolution sends weapons clattering to the floor. Swords point in all directions, spread out across the chancel interior and altar steps.

By now the mask has slogged down those same steps with lugubrious damp thuds. It clutches Arthur's foot. The patron kicks at it, but the strong, sticky muscle holds onto the polished leather and inches up over the hem of his trousers. His knees and hands jerk as if fending off a giant slug. The thief twists with his cuffed wrist over Arthur's head and brings their clamped hands down at his side, binding the other's arms. The thief hooks his leg over Arthur's leg. They fall tumbling backward together.

Pinned atop the smaller man, Arthur prattles and pleads between panicked breaths. The dislocated face creeps up Arthur's thigh, slides with thick muscle over his belt, and lugs itself up toward his chest.

The art thief locks their cramped limbs as one and yells: "Relax. Relax!"

Arthur doesn't relax.

The thief speaks more softly anyway. The mask continues to climb.

"Let me tell you a story. There were once two brothers who broke out of the black city. You know, the city that eats itself. They were twins who didn't look alike, but you could tell they were brothers by asking about the war. They'd always give you the same answer. And they liked a lot of the same things, the same girls, but since they didn't look like twins, they could never share things or play pranks the way twins do. The older they got, the more jealous of each other they grew. One twin was good and one twin was bad, but both of them wanted what the other one had. So now, I ask you, good twin or bad twin, which twin were you?"

The mask's slimy foot clenches and slides, convulsing as it

climbs Arthur's throat. His whole body feels cold. The suffocating massage makes him choke.

"Answer me, Arthur. Ha-ha."

Covering his chin, the gastropod mask grips Arthur's lower lip. As his skin stretches, he tastes salt in the velvety slime that seeps into his mouth. He tries to spit, but the thick slug grabs onto his top lip and seals off his mouth. Muffled underneath, Arthur's screams turn to gurgles: "Neither. Nob twin. Helb me. Mmmlb."

"Do you know how snails have sex?" The art thief holds Arthur's limbs in an inescapable knot. The mask keeps climbing higher on Arthur's silenced face, over his nostrils and up his cheeks, tugging the helpless skin under his eyes. "They twist their bodies together and hang in a fluorescent twirling kind of slime, melding hermaphroditically, trading bodies, doing it for hours and hours on end. It looks like some strange undersea flower or tumor, like if intestinal cancer ascended to Heaven instead of Elijah. It's beautiful beyond belief. The closest thing to angel-fucking you could ever imagine, brother. The world is full of such secrets."

Then the art thief disentangles his legs and arms and pushes Arthur off, striving to get upright despite the handcuffs holding them in tandem. He ends up on his hands and knees. Arthur lies immobile and slack. The black mask of blood with its five flames of gore engulfs his entire face.

Inside, with little light, sounds leach in from a distance as if underwater. Arthur feels less history and shame inside the smothering face, or does he, he wonders? No, not quite less. Ashamed as before for history, for unspoken crimes, for crimes indefinable and unnamed, this shared shame is more private. The soft muscular suction of the stolen face now his intimate companion, as close to shame as a sibling, as close to history as air.

He wonders how he can breathe and then notices the tugging of epithelial cilia spreading and dilating his nostrils. The wet slime of the snail foot lubricates what it covers, enabling Arthur to move his nose, his lips, and open and close his eyes. He reassures himself everything is okay; everything will be fine; he's not really smothering, not in any excessive pain. The mask must want him alive.

"Come on, buddy. Let's get a move on and take what's ours."
The art thief rattles their wrists. "Get on up."

Arthur blinks as he adjusts to the muted light and the blur of
mucus coating his eyes. He doesn't need to blink, so he ceases. Now
that his eyes are always open, all the clipped-out split seconds of life
he's lost to tiny blackouts while blinking come back amassed in a
flood of desire and regret.

And there it is; a subtle glow, like clouded piss. The sulfur light
of the salt cathedral's many screens oozes through the stolen face
achieving perfect clarity. Arched like gothic cathedral windows,
stretching the length of an impossibly long gallery in the nave along
the aisles, the screens take shape from a gel-like substance secreted
by the organism.

Arthur understands through his unwilling communion that the
cathedral is a type of worm, a salt-based organism masquerading as a
building. A thing long-buried and brought to life, or perhaps an idea
of a thing, exhumed by the sculptors and architects who carved out
this cathedral where it lay hidden, waiting to eat its way into organic
life; a digestive tunnel perforating time in an abandoned salt mine
two-thousand miles below a black lake.

Here in the naturally temperate chambers of crypts of salt, over
a century of unseen films and deleted sequences are housed, arcane
reliquary objects kept safe from the decaying action of warm air, the
restless nibbling of rats, and the destructive humidity that lurks
above ground. The cool, arid conditions perfect for preservation
helped the cathedral come to life. Fed or made hungry by the lost,
cursed, and expurgated contents of its chapels, contaminated by
discarded human dreams, the salt worm continually destroys the
footage, digesting it, assimilating it, dreaming the films deep in the
earth with a cross-like transept of vestigial appendages at its center
and apsidal compartments radiating outward like multiple pros-
tomium from the crown of its blind and luminous head. The
ingested human dreams live only in the white worm's cells, doubling
in darkness, communicable chemically through the gel secreted on
the walls of its intestine in the shape of cathedral windows. Perhaps,
Arthur thinks, the only way to view the archive is to submit to
digestion.

In the mask, Arthur can see the arch-shaped screens clearly, unlike the thief, who remains blinded by the cathedral's brightness. The corridor of intestine stretches longer than the gallery nave they first entered. The space has expanded. Arthur feels the worm soul within him stretch in sympathy with the surrounding organism, feels the illusion of flesh exposed in the docent transfigured above, her connective tissue vaulting the worm's ceiling and draping languidly in a flayed chandelier dripping with light. He tastes the salty exudate dissolving in his mouth beneath the mask and rises to reach for the secreted screens. This is what he came for.

As he stands, the cathedral turns upside down. The patron and the thief walk forward in reflection. One cannot go without the other; one cannot stay without the other. This mutual reversal is their intractable path.

Beneath a black lake, two brothers escape the city of Vantablack salt. By inversion, the city melts into liquid, spires rippling downward into an underground reversed city visible and inhabitable only through the shimmering movement of surface waves. The night around the brothers or lovers is a wet thing, slick with reflected images of cancerous air above. They breathe as if underwater, cruising through liquid. Mediated through the mask, the patron finds a natural rhythm in the burning and quenching of ozone going in and out of his lungs.

The art thief chokes. Bubbles erupt from his mouth. He gestures as if he would swim, arms flapping, cheeks puffing in and out. The patron pulls him closer to the rippling surface of the lake, the arch-shaped lake on the cathedral wall contained objectively as a window, and yet also subjectively vast and both containing and encompassing the two escaped men within its depths. The threshold for differentiation bleeds until the window turns black like the mask on Arthur's face. He pushes the gasping thief's back against the liquid pane and places the mask's mouth on the man's lips. Crushed in a kiss, the art thief falls backward into the screen. Together the brothers sink below the black lake and drown.

Around them, the city lights blur and tremble, broken by the shudder of small waves wafting downward in a continuous loop. The shimmer feels eternal in the night's stillness above. Inverted towers proliferate, pointed apexes made visible only by the choppy glint of their distant windows blinking in and out as the waves come and go, warp and weft. Electric emissions undergo a metamorphosis into bioluminescent mirage as the rays penetrate into the deep where the art thief and Arthur sink, mouth to mask to mouth.

The illusion of privacy in darkness embraces them, warmer than death. Arthur holds the smaller man tight and close. The thief thinks maybe he should fight, but he needs Arthur to breathe, to survive. Arthur also knows he should let go, but revels in the excuse. Something true discovers a new voice in their shared passionate thought: *I need him to survive.*

Thus the torment of secrecy and the joy of recognition binds them as brothers in deleted scenes. The lost film depicting a pair of rival twin serial murderers, a brotherhood forged through primal fantasy fuels their immersive kiss, as invasive as fucking, as powerful as beating a brother's head with a stone. In the sacrificial drama before the great flood, the lovers contend to martyr the most potent gift. Vying for the saliva of their absent father, who prefers his meat charred, escalating in violence, courting through increasingly gory performative risks, burning and feeding until the only worthy targets of torture are one another. The brothers' erotic bond transcends the first rule written on their hearts from birth: in incestuous sports of narcissistic competition, the winner always drowns.

Is this a game we played as children?

Arthur ponders as his mask breathes life back into his dead brother, or perhaps the film runs backwards, reversing his death. The footage ends, and having ingested what it needs of them through its toxic poetic message, it spits them out through the trembling gelatinous screen into the dry intestine of the cathedral nave. The patron and the art thief splash down with a surge of black water, landing on the glowing yellow floor carved of salt below the surface of the earth.

The thief coughs. Even as he catches his breath, bits of memory exit him, leaving no more than scattered biological traces of slick liquid, a melted city burning his skin, a suspicion of shared sickness, and ropey threads of congealed exhaust like phlegm or smegma lining his throat. He hacks up a clot. The meaning of it is vanishing too fast. The black gobbet hurled up from his lungs is something he can never sell.

"We can work together," he says between gasps. "This doesn't need to be your revenge arc for you to come out ahead." His slender frame seems more angular than ever, almost frail. Though he gives the impression of a young trickster at first glance, age and depredation break through in wiry striations across his cheekbones, veins, and hair. Arthur sees him differently now. Markings on the external soul's surface: tiger growing dim.

Concave posture and chest heaving, the art thief says: "We can both win. I'm a professional, okay? Remember what I said about the kingdom of Heaven?"

Arthur wants to answer that all he ever wanted was for everyone to love him, his brother first and most of all, but he'd have to remove the mask to speak and he's not ready for that, not sure if he can. Isn't it enough he just saved his life? But who is this man? Not his brother. Not his twin. That's an illusion of the Lost Museum, a consequence of some piece of his mind being digested and becoming not him but an artifact. Arthur will not be a man in the end but an archive of lost footage cut from notorious films like *Derelict Games*, also known as *Genesis*, a homoerotic retelling of the legend of Cain and Abel, infamous for its reputed snuff sequences and incest, starring two real-life twins who disappeared after filming. Released straight to VHS and quickly banned, all prints of it were destroyed when adolescent twins from several wealthy families in the Midwest reenacted its heinous climax.

None of this could have anything to do with Arthur's real life. *Derelict Games* could not be a real film, or else he would have heard of it. Arthur would remember if he murdered anyone or had sex with his brother. And how could he possibly forget dying of asphyxiation in an erotic suicide pact?

Then again, he thinks, *how would I remember?*

His solid belly and full chest feel heavy with responsibility for the corrosive visual text and the victims lost to its myth.

The thief says, "We're the kingdom, man. It's you and me, trapped in the dark with the same dream."

Arthur doesn't know what to believe. The organism writhes,

undulating beneath their feet, transporting them by contractions along its slippery intestine toward the chancel, the crown. The blood-brain barrier leads into deeper secrets. Arthur dreads visiting more forbidden wings of the museum.

Maybe it's not up to us, both Arthur and the art thief think, not yet knowing the thought is simultaneous, a biological consequence of the shared vision and eroticized rivalry pupating from the infamous censored film. The narrative takes root, a parasite in the would-be brothers. Or are the men separate parasites in this creature, this temple, this place of insides?

Another shared thought: *Far enough; we have to find a way out.*

"I'm not leaving here empty-handed," says the art thief, wrist raw, arm limp, cuffed to the larger man who looms silent in the blood-blackened mask. "You never even asked me my name."

Arthur tries to speak. He wants to ask, wants to know after all they've suffered and shared. When his lips part, muscle-thick mucous like another tongue slips into his mouth. Salt and flower-like slickness coat his palette, his tonsils, the passageway into his stomach or spleen or lungs. He's not sure how his insides are arranged, whether they're the same or altered since passing through the gelatinous screens. He moves his mouth parts and diaphragm in a pattern that should ask: "What's your name?" What comes out of the mask-hole is a deafening metallic squeal, an inhuman siren, a honking signal saturated by empty bombastic excess.

The vaulted ceiling reverses as though activated by sound. The arches point down, forming like stalactites; the organism is a cave, and the docent transfigured above now droops into many udders. Dangling low, obstructing the restricted wing of The Lost Museum, the docent's skeins of flayed skin drip impossibly, stretched and cumbersome, bags of fluid too swollen for the thief and the patron to navigate through against their tumescent weight. Her single navel eye blinks once and becomes a mouth.

"Our next exhibit is an assemblage from *The Most Important Dress of the Twenty-Third Century*, a documentary transmitted illegally from the future, captured by an anonymous cable TV production assistant, said to expose the controversy surrounding an unexpected metamorphosis of fetal-sourced skins grown in lab culture that resulted in sentient fabric."

Muffled cacophony from elsewhere punctuates her monotone oration with what might be vomiting or laughter. Arthur is distracted by the volatile noise, unable to follow the narrative. The docent's dress swells and sags with increasing weight, grazing against cheek and mask. The elongated fluid sacs undulate like an upended sea anemone swayed by waves. Fabric tendrils seek the men out by imitating natural motion, softening as they bloat.

The texture of the tendrils feels like the skin of a peach and a newborn's head. Warm from an increasing fluid burden, they invite touch. The art thief reaches up, overcome by fascination, his uncuffed hand playing on the responsive surface, lips brushing the skin as it grows more wet and plush. His bound hand crushes into Arthur's stomach as the swaying udders encircle and press them together, closing in a soft yet impenetrable ring.

Arthur's mask excludes him from similar enjoyment. He cringes from the cloying udders or tendrils, senses the skin thinking about him, wanting him. He dislikes the deliberate shifting pressure of contained liquid as the sacs mold to his shoulders, his ass, the backs of his knees. Swollen weight crowds and then shifts away, seeking intimacy. The warm damp of each caress leaves Arthur clammy.

Immobilized, he can't evade the insistent clutching and nudging, can't stop the sick blare of laughter and vomiting that still echoes from elsewhere hidden within the head of the demented cathedral. Surely the worm has gone mad from eating its own dreams. Too many dreams in the crush of the demanding dress; too many appetites in the fabric's sentient skin. Arthur endures all the folds and hideous contact while the art thief suckles and tugs at an udder that responds by elongating further and leaking more fluid. The undulating sac pulsates against the thief's torso. It rubs between his legs.

The art thief bites into the fabric and white fluid spurts into his mouth. So much fluid the thief can't swallow it all. White dribbles down his chin. His throat convulses with effort. The emptying udder thins and curls around him, its teat orifice opening and closing like an excited sphincter. He mounts it, feeding and fucking all at once.

Arthur can't pull away. Fearful he risks being fully digested the longer the film runs, brain matter decayed and identity subsumed by its dementia-ridden myths, in forced proximity Arthur has no choice but to participate. He's splashed by fluid, yanked back and forth by the other man's fucking, any protest or warning silenced by the salty constriction of the black mask of congealed blood that holds tight to his face no matter how hard he's tossed to and fro. The snail foot grips, sealing his whimpering lips. Subjected to the other man's ecstasy, Arthur retches at the sour perfume of the white fluid. He wonders what's wrong with him for feeling disgust, and wishes he had a body with such capacity for pleasure.

The thief's orgasm shudders against Arthur's side like a fever. The dress unwinds. Arthur cries, or he would cry if the mask allowed it. The ache of rising tears seeps up from his stomach and into his chest. A sharp pain stalls in his gullet, spreading inward with a sensation like swallowing a rock. The gastropod grip on his visage holds. Unable to express his tears or howl in despair, his anguish spreads from the thick knot in his throat and radiates across his shoulders in a suffocating ache. He's afraid he's having a heart attack.

The thief snores in contentment. Arthur collapses. The dress eases them down together, slithering, growing sticky, snaking open along new seams. Satisfied by its seduction, the sentient fabric changes to a new predatory texture. Though it still billows with sensuous liquid folds, the surface now cuts like sandpaper, editing what it despises, shifting fluid and fat to feminize the thief's flesh on contact.

He grows thick hips and full breasts under its abrading edges. His cheeks plump up. His mouth makes a doll-shaped oh as he stirs wanly and gasps. Like a bloodless C-section cut, the fabric scissors open the thief's groin and abdomen and begins pooling inside, shaping a new cavity within his unconscious body, a large belly pregnant with a litter of dresses.

The udders have all emptied. Arthur's soaking wet and not sure how to breathe. The mask makes the necessary airways expand and contract. His chest pain solidifies, as if the rock he swallowed has swallowed his heart. Inside, the hungry stone is a permanent heart attack. Beside him, the leftover limp sacs of fabric gather in a damp mob, clinging, draping, and inflating the sleeping thief.

The dress is the same substance as the arch-shaped screens, the windows of living exudate made of censored and cursed dreams. Arthur no longer needs to see the lost footage playing out on its reflective surface because he can feel the liquid film seeping into his skin and through his clothes as the gelatinous fabric overflows, operating, inseminating, altering the man next to him who he's helpless to protect.

The dress blinks. This is not a surprise. The circumcising eye in the vaulted docent that was once a navel and now a mouth opens this time as a cervix. It is of the same fabric as the dress, colorless, bloodless, a pallid tone of illicit and empty white. In the illegal documentary, formal gowns swoop from the cervix like paper swans. They escape the lab, reproducing in the wild, smothering habitat and snagging wildlife in their sequined nets. The brothers, recruited as bounty hunters, slaughter the errant garments to near extinction. In the twenty-third century, the murderous twins are first praised for controlling an invasive species and later vilified for decimating a new and unique form of life. Pundits argue over the ethical dilemma. The film is blatant propaganda.

Supporters chant: "Rend the veils!"

"Misogyny! Genocide! Witch hunt!" decry the pro-dress activists. In an unwitting twist on *The Emperor's New Clothes*, many towns have ousted humans from power and elected sentient dresses to serve on city council with eyes on governor's seats. Naked rebels rounded up by dress rights advocates go into breeding camps.

In one such camp, the brothers make their suicide pact.

The art thief writhes, awakening bound. Mummified into forced womanhood, he flinches with the flutter of each fertilized egg inside the spaces between his cells. He feels his organs overpopulated and his body about to burst. The last thing he remembers is the most monumental fuck of his life, and now he is a pregnant carcass that belongs to someone else. The invasive fabric, like sticky foreskin, builds an unrecognizable colony of his destroyed genitals. He doesn't recognize what he's looking at. When the intense pressure within makes him piss himself, he can't tell where the wetness comes out. He can't control where it goes and he's helpless to stop.

He sobs.

He's not my brother; a thought springs from deep inside Arthur's gut. The chaos of the film's demands mixed with the strong urine smell reminding him of something held dear but forgotten. No memory, only the sweetness of the mood haunts him. *I don't even know this man or anything about him*, Arthur thinks. With great sadness, Arthur admits he wants to know him, remembers kissing him, and wants to kiss again. Without the mask, without pretext. Arthur must make a decision but he decides not to decide, not about morality, not about theft, and not about whose salvation or death changes the direction of history.

The thief weeps in his confused and agitated state, bound in the newly changed fabric flesh. Arthur grapples and lifts him, though the handcuffs make it difficult to maneuver. He stands up, and with a grunt hoists the thief up over his head.

Arm bent strangely to his attached wrist, afraid he'll piss on the man lifting him, afraid he'll be dropped or thrown, the thief stammers and says, "Hey, look, man; I don't care what you've done, okay? This is all cinema; fake places and fake people where no one gets arrested. The real shit happens off-screen. I know there are people in the real world, but I don't know how those people live. They can't pay because they're already in prison. Down here, man, down here it's all meat."

It's just you and me, right?"

Sometimes, Arthur wants to say, *sometimes you fall in love, and there's nothing you can do to stop it.* And he's surprised by the consequences of letting this thought speak, even though the mask emits no words but only the same horrific and brittle metallic shriek.

The five flames of gore glow hot at the tips like melting glass, turning from black to yellow to blue. Above Arthur's head, reacting to the extreme heat, the womanskin weeps, desiccating over the course of time. Mummified fabric flaps in senile rags as crisp as paper. Yellowing, shrinking, collating, crumbling, the ancient book of the thief remains bound to Arthur's wrist in a child-sized sarcophagus. The book grows lighter as the fat drips down Arthur's raised arms. Unborn offspring will suffer within its pages, thoughts forever unable to take form.

Snippets of the screenplay that remain legible in the raised host will be unknowable to anyone but Arthur, whose mind has become a thief through knowing. Those who read will not understand. *Seek and you will keep seeking. Knock and you will be made a door.*

Charred, the book brings an acrid smell of overcooked flesh as Arthur's lowers it to his chest. The book as Eucharist, as body both dead and active, as pieta in Arthur's arms. He brings the book of the thief to his lips. The lips are not his, but his mask's. The speaking image refuses to speak.

No docent in the vaulted ceiling offers guidance. Pallid vulva molded of stone recall her presence in decorative motifs. Dress and skin sacrificed, her discarded anatomy sculpts the archways of the roof in elaborate arrangements of bone. Through the skeletal patterns, veins thread, weave, and clot into colorful windows like stained glass. Fluids pool, but no images or emotions emerge. No exudate gels into a narrative. Arthur opens the book of his brother, the book of his guilt, and reads out loud in the salt-carved intestine as the vaulted muscle and ligament of the organism flexes.

The mask's metallic rasp summons the dead god-thing edited out of the final script. It removes the art thief from history, and makes public Arthur's private dialogue with his brother's image, giving rise to many arguments, activating many symbols, speaking truth to fear. And now, accepting all levels of paradox, as the laughter and vomiting and orgiastic howls erupt again and echo louder and wilder from the neural center of the diseased organism's head, Arthur crosses the blood-brain barrier of the salt cathedral's altar and takes his position in the exhibit on the Lost Museum's most hidden and cursed stage.

A hush falls over the histrionic space. The closed set is bathed in red light. The cameras are rolling, as they have been since before Arthur manifested. Actors and sex workers in prosthetic gore hold their tableau. The book of the thief rests on an altar of contortionists, three nudes erotically entwined in a complicated geometry of pene-tration and sensual caress to form a solid block from their supple bodies. The director has just finished reading from the book. Black candles and other absurd occult detritus surround him. Amazed, he gapes at Arthur, his eyes chaotic with shock, delight, and dread.

More powerful than a hand of glory, the book of the thief comes from the whole body of an immolated felon. Bound to its twin, the book is said to bring the devil back from infinity. The nameless man in the substance of its pages has been released by fire from the narrative flow of time, able to reach a listener in the future and speak in the past and collide with the present through the void. The young director didn't entirely believe or understand its power, even upon touching the thief's burnt corpse in the crisp black binding of the book.

Arthur is the devil. His heartbreak is impossible to describe, his guilt like a rod in his throat. The mask like a crime on his face clings with the strength of betrayal. His summoning is complete. The film is cursed.

Those who enter the hidden wing of the Lost Museum will not watch. They will see. They will step onto the stage and into the salt cathedral's brain as victims sworn to secrecy on the closed set. No one remains in the audience, for indifference is impossible. Viewing invokes a conversion of flesh to film. The deleted footage from *Blood Orgy* will not exist but will continue to grow, forever accumulating bodies and expanding in detail and length as the knowledge of its lost torture sequence spreads. None will watch. They will see. Those who see, become.

"We killed the wrong god," says the book.

Everyone on the set gasps. The shocked stillness following Arthur's sudden manifestation breaks. The red-lit assembly scrambles, babbling, seeking escape, clawing at the edges of the set. Where once there were walls, now a bleak abyss; a blurred uncertainty meets their hands. Something chews away the skin and flesh of fingers, flaying hands, arms, and wrists, except there's nothing there: they chew themselves. They ingest the darkness, their own flesh, each other, the idea of darkness. They bring the void inside. Every bite out of the blurred edge expands its circumference.

The set is endless, with endless room for atrocity and self-mutilation. At its center, Arthur's heart is ill beyond the reach of compassion, wishing he could undo his brother's death.

The book speaks once more.

"Madness is what we've lost. The kingdom of heaven is a mutating cell that begs for transformation. Its violence is the opposite of war, a counterpoint to sacrifice, and the miracle of visceral emotions that force us into a necessary and personal dialogue with the angels we've trapped. Every biological process is another useless passion play reifying history."

Heeding his brother's voice, Arthur must cry again. He must crack away the dried black blood mask and come again. He splits it with his fist by smashing his septum and pries away the shards, tearing through the moist under-flesh. The strong muscle of the gastropod holds on below the five flames of gore that rise from his forehead. He claws at the soft-bodied muscle, ripping away chunks of his face to extract it, mangling his face as he murders the snail foot, the mask meat, the soft underbelly of the thing he has always pretended to be.

Flames wild on his forehead, Arthur's face bleeds.

He sees with his own eyes.

Time funnels like a spiral through the spinning reels. The salt cathedral keeps the eyes it tastes in perpetuity through digestive juices. Eyes dissolved into secreted gel on the worm's intestinal walls, digestion spreading the blood vision, the Hell vision, the fire vision, the sick vision, the harm vision, the lost vision. The eyeless vision is the kingdom within.

The madness increases as the void expands inside bodies like a virus, outside like a black hole. The floor blooms liquid with beatings. Human voices squeal like things in a slaughterhouse, crying with Arthur's agony and emptiness. Death-cries are sex-cries, keening in need of abuse. Desperate to be hurt and filled, the once-human things keep thrusting and eating, escalating in intensity long after the meat of them should have ejaculated or expired. Wounds proliferate and open, violated by genitals, fists, or hacked off stumps. No eye socket is safe, no patch of skin un-slashed.

The hunger for self-harm agitates cravings for hammers, bindings, hangings by electrical cord, for any butchery possible with the equipment and rigging on set. With each straining blow, a man on the ground raises a steel pipe above his head and grimaces in fierce pleasure. Even as his breath shudders with the onset of physiological shock, he slams the pipe down on his shins over and over. His cock jerks when the pipe makes contact. Cracking through bone, pulverizing heel and calf, he makes a stew of his lower legs.

Stringy sinew splatters out raw in a broth of blood. A circle of onlookers masturbate, urging him on. Men stand and stroke while those already castrated lap at the feast spreading on the floor. The man's veins strain. His arms shake. He grunts. Finally he drops the pipe and vomits onto his lap, sperm shooting up through the chunks from his climax and raining down thick from his audience.

Several disheveled women hoist him by the armpits and drag him away. They grab the steel pipe to press against his throat, another to shove inside him. Shreds of ligament and knee break off behind his ruined legs. Semen, smashed bone, crushed vein, and torn muscle tissue smear those who crawl or slide in reptilian adulation, gulping and grinding, cutting with bone fragments in the slurry. They feast upon the mutilated remnants of the man's legs and then upon each other.

Mouths overstuffed with raw fat and still-bleeding flesh clamp over bleeding cocks. Someone gnaws through their own forearm and shoves the ulna up their ass. Teeth demolish rippling buttocks, leaving gaping holes. An overfed throat chokes as it tears into a muscular vulva convulsing with such ecstatic force that the owner's skull is crushed.

The book catalogues the horrors, numerous and varied, for it is the task of any museum to maintain a complete and detailed index of its collection, and to secure the provenance of every exhibit. Chained to the book, Arthur reads the unthinkable language decomposing its text from tiny worms that bore through the pages and writhe on the surface as script. Smaller than human pores, they slide in through palms and fingertips. They strip information, forcing eye movements that corrupt neural pathways like prions, boring holes in the brain of the seeker. The more one searches for meaning or narrative, the less there is.

Arthur falls to his knees. The human altar beside him heaves and strains to penetrate deeper inside one another. Knotted in an elaborate fuck, body parts probe and gouge, pushing until tangled limbs, wounds, and orifices fuse into a single block of sweating flesh. The smell of body fluids, spoiled meat, and rancid cum rise up. Across the altar, the director also kneels, first as a dumb mimic, and now collapsing as a beast in frolic, rolling in the altar's discharge.

The director laughs an empty wormhole laugh. He has read the book. Vacuoles of nothingness tunnel through him like the appendages of the great white worm that tunnel through the geological body of the earth.

"We have nothing to fear," the director cackles without humor. "Hell is only a word." Gulping and hiccoughing as he laughs like a thing stabbed and airless, a once-human balloon braying as it turns itself inside-out, he gags his own throat with his whole forearm and claws inside his rib cage to grab his heart. His torso convulses around the arm, jerking with smothered belly laughs.

He pulls his heart out through his mouth with a loud series of sucking and popping sounds. The glistening organ gushes one last vital flood and slumps. He raises it, damp in his cupped palms, and brings it back up toward his open mouth, hungering, salivating, anticipating with demonic lust.

Arthur cries out, "I never wanted any of this." He turns away, close to tears, face weeping blood. The film jams, freezing the director in place. The moaning chaos goes silent. It's so quiet the devil can hear himself breathe.

The problem is twofold. The footage is in poor condition. Furthermore, the set has lost all architectural logic. Encrusted with layers of gore, *Blood Orgy* is a grotesquerie of mangled parts exploded into unrecognizable pulp by the sadomasochistic feast of rape and mutilation. Walls so thickly slathered emit no light. As the salt cathedral slips into a coma, the organism no longer thinks or screens. The dreams in the digestive gel have begun to digest themselves.

The book of the thief speaks softly. "We'll never dream alone again once the lights go out. When you think of me, you'll feel nothing, only emptiness. You won't remember my name or what we've meant to each other. You'll forget our love, like it never happened. You won't even know you had a brother, or a father, or a son."

"Please don't say things like that."

"This is the end, where you realize nothing you said or did ever mattered. And more than that; your suffering didn't matter. All the pain you went through was just another illusion you decided to believe. There's always a choice. Do you ever ask yourself why you dumped so much money into making this place?"

Arthur crouches and trembles, clutching the book close to his chest, shaking, yet still not able to cry. "This isn't my fault. I'm just a donor, like my father."

"Our father. And we don't have one anymore. That's the problem with twins. They eat all the leftovers."

"I'll die here, won't I? This is the end, isn't it?"

"You're oversimplifying the situation. We turned a mountain upside down to fill a valley with the sun, like filling a cup; we drank the sun all day long until the nighttime stars woke up."

The book of the thief sings instead of speaking the last few phrases. Out of place in the mad gut of the salt worm cathedral, the familiar music is more of a shock than the cannibal orgy stench and frozen tableaus of torture surrounding Arthur. Within the white worm's brain, Arthur holds his brother and sings the rest of the song.

Rhymes and melodies they made up as children, simplistic verses with plots borrowed from cartoons and comics giving way to more serious lyrics as they aged. Through rivalries, games, reconciliations, and betrayals, they wove verse upon verse, adding to the adventure tale of two brothers, until one day, something between them changed.

It's impossible to pinpoint exactly when it happened and why the singing stopped. As Arthur recalls the long, silly, wandering song, the melody resonates easily from his throat as if his breath and muscles had been waiting for this moment. Though he hasn't thought of it since childhood, the song pours out.

He rocks the nameless man against his chest. The tears he couldn't cry come out in excess. At the end of the song, it stops mid-verse without any sense of closure, abandoned suddenly by the brothers. Soaked, the book of the thief drips worms and ink. If the text was ever readable, it no longer instructs, nor does it sing. It hangs limp on the end of the chain from Arthur's wrist, soggy and small like an excised tattoo.

At the end of the film, one brother bleeds and the other one burns. Both are guilty. Nobody talks about the war. The dream of the body and the covenants it performs are a shell around the true center of nothingness, a suicidal center Arthur must enter alone. Below the surface, between the cells, behind the names, all are equally nameless and alone, both brothers and planets alike are seasoned in the void and unmade by shared dreaming. Christ calls you to die and the devil tempts you to live, but the footage of the primal scene has been censored. Corrupted by the gut of the salt queen, it will never be restored.

The queen worm cathedral has laid eggs in her death throes, microscopic beads on the underside of reality. Arthur's tears crust into a cavern of salt. Bones of the organism spin in vaulted arches above him. A sea of viscera wells up from below.

He bites through the chain, breaking his teeth. He tugs the ragged remains of the book free and folds the disintegrating pages into his jacket pocket. Crossing the living altar, he stops the director's heart. Reaching into the scene with both hands, he clasps the soggy organ between his palms, pulls it away from the rabid mouth of the madman, and walks backward and away.

The chain sways as he steps, still draped from his wrist. Heart held out in front of his eyes, Arthur doesn't turn around to see where he's going. There's no point. No way out of the edgeless void, no direction to check. He bares his unmasked face to the torn-out organ. Like mangled mirrors, the devil's face and the injured heart share a similar ravaged crimson pall and an irreversible woundedness.

By gazing into the mirror wound of the torn heart at the center of the stage where he was summoned, Arthur solves the mystery of the closed set. Traversing the blood-brain barrier backward, he exits from *Blood Orgy* and into the nave where the red and black darkness is dispelled, enveloped in the intestine's yellow light.

Within the organism, decay spreads. Salt walls crumble. Saffron-colored dust floats in thick motes in the air. The digestive gel of the dream-windows desiccates and peels, thin as tissue paper, flaking off like gold leaf. Remnants of the docent sag in the vaulted ceiling, honey-colored and disintegrating in a slow drip. Arthur backs down the altar steps, continues past the choir and transept, and ends up where he came in at the doors of the narthex.

He wants to believe each step backward reverses some damaged dream and seals another wound in the self-mutilated carcass of the real. The heart pressed tight between his palms, he exerts more force with each step, pushing harder with both hands. The heart like a planet, his hands like the sky containing it, keeping it from unravelling with each refusal to look away. Finally crushing the director's heart with enough geological force to compress it into a large gemstone with a fierce red glow, Arthur holds a treasure at the threshold known as the Egg of Hell.

The heist is nearly complete, but the stress on his wrists has opened old scars. White-lipped slashes spit blood like false apologies. The scar-smeared lips remind Arthur why he spent his fortune amassing a collection and housing it in the Lost Museum.

"We made this place to be together," the left wrist sings to the right wrist.

"From now on, we'll never dream alone," the right wrist sings to the left. "We can stay here, trapped alone together, in the dark."

Arthur accepts responsibility for the film's failure. He didn't cut deep enough.

The scars sing the epic melody the brothers invented as children, but with new verses, new words. Exsanguinating voices drain Arthur's veins. One brother bleeds and one brother burns, and Arthur has not yet bled enough. Like a film gutted of subtext, unwilling to acknowledge or confront its obsession with repetitive imagery of self-harm, the voices sing away his eyes in fierce denial. He can't keep them open, growing lightheaded. The new words are in the contagious worm language from the book, the singing scars like worms stretching across the long-healed ridges of his childhood cuts.

He slumps against a pillar and drops down to put his head between his knees. His forehead cracks on the Egg of Hell. The five flames of gore protruding from his scalp sear the fissure shut before the jelly leaks out. With a sudden flash of insight, Arthur lifts his wrists to the flames to cauterize the mouths. He hesitates, not in fear of pain, but because to stop the bleeding means the song will be cut short. The recovered melody will be silenced and Arthur will be back where he started before entering the Lost Museum. The song of the two brothers will return to being unfinished and forgotten.

And so he listens a little longer.

I've been bleeding to death since I was born, Arthur thinks. *The time to stop it was twenty years ago.* He rests his hands on his lap, wrist-up on each thigh, one on the right and one on the left. They sing him past the mountain, through the city, beneath the inverted surface of the black lake, and into salt cathedral of The Lost Museum. One brother bleeds and the other one burns, and neither of their stories makes sense without the other. The devil summoned, half of him already here in the charred flesh of the book, the other half trimmed in service of the wrong god. No one will speak openly of this once the records are purged.

The Egg of Hell glows between Arthur's knees. He basks in the blur of its light.

From outside, sounds intersperse with his song. Footsteps and voices. Arthur faintly hums along through final verses taking the long-lost brothers through *Derelict Games* to *The Most Important Dress of the Twenty-Third Century* to the *Blood Orgy* exhibit and then back here to the starting place where it's time to pay. The edges of his vision blink out.

He'll wait for his brother. Isn't that his playful reprobate voice he hears at the entrance, asking, "What danger?"

New visitors approach the narthex. They cross the threshold and enter the dream.

"The architecture of the salt cathedral is known in local lore as an angel trap. A circle-preserving transformation composed of an even number of inversions, not unlike the mechanisms powering the heart of a minotaur. I warn you, whatever your intentions: the body has its own logic."

Footsteps, confusion, disruption; a new voice, frightened and sallow: "History isn't done with us. No more light. Please."

"Let's make some room for joy in your life," his brother says, handcuffed to Arthur's wrist. The last verse of the song plays out, revealing the story has two endings. Darkness presses down like a hand closing a corpse's eyes. Arthur knows the other's presence by the warmth at his side, the pulsing of breath, and the shared sensation of a threshold within a threshold. By the time the singing stops, all that remains perceptible is the Egg of Hell glowing in his lap.

The red gem throbs, keeping time with the melody after it ends. Veins emerge on the surface. By irregular degrees of gradual faceted expansion, the shell grows translucent. Subdermal cracks spread like the eager licking motion of a fire. Something pushes outward, thinning the shell.

Arthur feels it rumble around him as the salt cathedral expands and contracts. The Lost Museum will carve holes into the earth until the caves collapse the planet. The worst dreams of self-mutilation and sexual torture inverted through a wormhole, meaninglessness devouring meaninglessness. The organism's death un-melts the black lake and locks the gates of the city of Vantablack salt.

What if there was a sky? Arthur thinks as his extremities grow colder. *What if outside this tunnel with its infinite holes, there wasn't more darkness, but a sky to encircle the mad disintegrating brain of the planet with hands of light, to clasp it, and hold it together?*

His hands lie palm up as if to receive or give an offering. He turns them weakly toward the light and fire spreading across the hardened shell. Maybe they'll burn on contact. Maybe he won't have enough strength. He matches the curve of his palms to the slope of the shell and begins to push. As the yellow fissures in the Egg of Hell become deepening black cracks, the shell splits in many places, breaking open innumerable surfaces and hatching the many secrets held within.

ACKNOWLEDGMENTS

It's impossible to thank everyone whose influence, contribution, or encouragement helped create these stories. It's even harder to acknowledge the help and influence of horrible people and situations that have challenged and strengthened me as a person and a writer. I think that's why I've never written acknowledgments before. Because adversity has been one of my greatest teachers, and I just couldn't get my words around it. So, to the people not yet dead who were horrible to me, you have a certain careful measure of my gratitude. No one is horrible in a vacuum. I was there too.

Now, for the fun part, the joyous thanks. Hailey Piper and Joseph Bouthiette Jr. have been there since the beginning of my writing attempts. Thank you for seeing my potential and getting others to have a look. Hailey, you've been a cheerleader, friend, and mentor, and I did nothing to deserve your bounty. Thank you.

Too many talented authors for my small mind to contain provided feedback, beta readings, or conversations about craft, form, and intention, boosting my confidence in the stories and helping me refine them to the best of my ability, such as it is. For the gift of their time and indulgence my thanks go to J. A. W. McCarthy, Donyae Coles, M. Lopes da Silva, Michael Tichy, Scott J. Moses, Sam Richard, Ira Rat, and to my anonymous and perhaps unwitting alien in a jar.

Thanks go to the editors who risked their reputations and dollars on my weirdness. I'm perpetually in shock that anything I write gets published. You're my heroes for giving me a home for my work and adding the finishing touches in final edits; thank you Mae, Joe, Kevin, Evan, Evan, Bobby, Alan, Alex, Chris, James, Andrew, Eric, Sam, Scott, and J.D.

Thank you unto my most beloved Vile Cesspool. Your rawfrog energy sustains me.

At this point, I'm worried I've forgotten someone. I know I've forgotten someone, and if that's you, I'm sorry. Remind me so I can make it up to you.

Finally, I'm truly thankful for each reader and reviewer who interacted with me or my writing over the past few years. The stories in this collection were mostly written during the pandemic, while dealing with isolation, and the extensive use of second person reflects how much I needed you. If you were listening, I sincerely can't thank you enough.

ABOUT THE AUTHOR

Joe Koch (he/they) writes literary horror and surrealist trash. Their books include *The Wingspan of Severed Hands, Convulsive,* and *The Couvade,* which received a Shirley Jackson Award nomination in 2019. His short fiction appears in numerous publications online and in print such as *Vastarien, Southwest Review, PseudoPod, Children of the New Flesh,* and *The Book of Queer Saints.* Joe also co-edited the art horror anthology *Stories of the Eye.* Though rarely spotted in the wild, Joe can be found online at horrorsong.blog.

PREVIOUS PUBLICATION
ACKNOWLEDGEMENTS

"Invaginies" –first published in *Children of the New Flesh: The Early Work and Pervasive Influence of David Croneneberg* from 11:11 Press, 2022

"Bride Of The White Rat" –first published in *Antifa Splatterpunk* from Cursed Morsels Press, 2022

"I Married A Dead Man" –first published in *What One Wouldn't Do* from Scott J. Moses, 2021

"Leviathan's Knot" –first published in *Into The Crypts of Rays: A Black Metal Horror Anthology, Volume II* from Castaigne Publishing, 2021

"Convulsive, Or Not At All" –first published in *In the Shadow of The Horns: A Black Metal Horror Anthology* from Castaigne Publishing, 2021

"Chironoplasty" –first published in Your Body Is Not Your Body from Tenebrous Press, 2022

"The Love That Whirls" –first published in *The Book of Queer Saints* from Mae Murray, 2022

"Oakmoss & Ambergris" –first published in *Three-Lobed Burning Eye Magazine, Issue 35*, 2022

"Reverend Crow" –first published in *Liminal Spaces* from Cemetery Gates Media, 2021

"Eclipse, Embrace" –first published in *Let the Weirdness In: A Tribute to Kate Bush* from Heads Dance Press, 2022

"I Tied Your Heart On A String" –first published in *Southwest Review, Volume 107, Number 4*, 2023

"Beloved Of Flies" –first published online by Action Books, 2022

"Five Visitations" –first published in *Campfire Macabre, Volume* 2 from Cemetery Gates Media, 2022

"Pigman, Pigman" –first published online by Cemetery Gates Media, 2021

"Studies After The Human Figure" –first published in *Ceci n'est pas une histoire d'horreur* from Night Terror Novels, 2021

"All The Rapes In The Museum" –first published in *Stories of the Eye* from Weirdpunk Books, 2022

"Coneland" –first published online by Shortwave Magazine, 2022

ALSO BY CLASH BOOKS

EVERYTHING THE DARKNESS EATS

Eric LaRocca

THE BODY HARVEST

Michael J. Seidlinger

FLOWERS FROM THE VOID

Gianni Washington

LETTERS TO THE PURPLE SATIN KILLER

Joshua Chaplinsky

THE KING OF VIDEO POKER

Paolo Iacovelli

VAGUE PREDICTIONS AND PROPHECIES

Daisuke Shen

DEATH ROW RESTAURANT

Daniel Gonzalez

THE BLACK TREE ATOP THE HILL

Karla Yvette

THE LONGEST SUMMER

Alexandrine Ogundimu

WE PUT THE LIT IN LITERARY

CLASHBOOKS.COM

FOLLOW US

IG
X
FB

@clashbooks

Printed in the USA
CPSIA information can be obtained
at www.ICGtesting.com
JSHW021322180624
64962JS00022B/42

9 781960 988119